Sonya was born in a small village to a single mother. Her life was hard, but she remained kind. Often helping those who needed it, without thought.

Making friends was difficult. Children are often cruel. She had only a few who she was close to.

Being shy and quiet throughout her life made things hard. Working several jobs from a young age, so she was able to buy the things her mother couldn't afford.
General to a fault.

Dedicated to those who have gone through life's hardships and survived.

Sonya J Wright

THE CIRCLE HOUSE

AUSTIN MACAULEY PUBLISHERS®

LONDON • CAMBRIDGE • NEW YORK • SHARJAH

A CIP catalogue record for this title is available from the British Library.

ISBN 9781035851355 (Paperback)
ISBN 9781035851362 (ePub e-book)

www.austinmacauley.com

First Published 2025
Austin Macauley Publishers Ltd®
1 Canada Square
Canary Wharf
London
E14 5AA

My family always believed that I could achieve anything. My man and his beautiful daughter both help me realise my worth every day. My friends have known me through good and bad times. They all helped me get here. I love you all.

Table of Contents

Prologue	**13**
Chapter One: Arrivals	**16**
Chapter Two: Room Three, Julie's Journey	**19**
Chapter Three	**24**
Chapter Four	**29**
Chapter Five	**35**
Chapter Six	**41**
Chapter Seven	**45**
Chapter Eight	**49**
Chapter Nine	**54**
Chapter Ten	**58**
Chapter Eleven: Room Nine, Duke's Story	**61**
Chapter Twelve	**64**
Chapter Thirteen	**70**
Chapter Fourteen	**75**
Chapter Fifteen	**79**

Chapter Sixteen   83

Chapter Seventeen   87

Chapter Eighteen   92

Chapter Nineteen   96

Chapter Twenty   101

Chapter Twenty-One   104

Chapter Twenty-Two: Room One, Amy's Journey   107

Chapter Twenty-Three   110

Chapter Twenty-Four   114

Chapter Twenty-Five   118

Chapter Twenty-Six   123

Chapter Twenty-Seven   130

Chapter Twenty-Eight   133

Chapter Twenty-Nine: Room Ten, Benny's Journey   136

Chapter Thirty   145

Chapter Thirty-One   149

Chapter Thirty-Two   153

Chapter Thirty-Three   157

Chapter Thirty-Four   162

Chapter Thirty-Five   167

Chapter Thirty-Six   171

Chapter Thirty-Seven   **177**

Epilogue   **180**

Prologue

Have you ever wondered how some things are not as they seem?

How a person can be the complete opposite to how they act?

When you think it is chicken that you are eating, it turns out to be something quite unexpected?

When you see something, you just know that it wasn't there before.

This is the place that makes you question, not only your sanity but also your existence, and the reality in which you were born.

Take a trip to somewhere that is out of the ordinary, shocking you out of your comfort zone, pulling you somewhere that will lead to your destiny, or doom.

Be warned, there is only one path to choose, one way in which to find what you are looking for. Challenging you and everything you thought was important.

The truth will always be found, and there shall only be the outcome that fits who you are, what you want to be and where you have been.

Choose a door, it will open to your own personal destination, but once you step inside, there is no turning back.

Come to The Circle House; open your mind to the impossible.

***

"Come on, you muppets. We are late already. The Circle House will not let us in."

It is hard for these four friends to relate to one another. They are so different in many ways.

The impatient one is Julie, with a temper and stubborn streak. She is hard to care about, but they do. Her sweet side is hidden from all but those closest to her. With long blond hair and striking green eyes, it's hard to imagine that she lacks self-esteem.

"Keep your cool, sexy lady. Your man is here."

That is Duke. He is not Julie's man, which is not to say this hyper and confident boy hasn't tried to be. With dark brown hair, hazel eyes and a face that should be on a magazine cover, he is shocked that Julie doesn't want him.

What is hidden behind all the confidence?

"OK, babes. I am ready. Who wants to drive first? Me? All right then."

That is the sweet and sexy Benny. A hunk of a man with a heart of gold, his cute dimples, dark blond hair and light blue eyes make him look angelic. He is in love with Amy. She is next on the list.

Does this man really have a heart of gold? We shall see.

"Sorry, I couldn't get my bag closed again. You know how mornings are for me, but here I am."

Now, we have Amy, beautiful and smart. Her long dark hair and electric blue eyes make a striking combination.

There is something about her that pulls people in. Is it because she does not hide who is inside?

Let us find out when they all choose a room and travel on their paths to insanity or redemption, only time will tell.

This is going to be fun…

Chapter One
Arrivals

Pulling up to the beautiful building, our group cannot help but admire the structure. Outside the place looks to be a flawless sphere. There are no windows or doors. The huge Circle Guesthouse sits on a white marble block. The sphere itself changes colour depending on how the light hits.

A door opens as the speechless guests approach. The opening is in the marble block, which has a blue light filtering out of it. Stairs led up to the open space.

As everyone ascends, a very tall and stunning woman approaches. With her black hair that is cut to a blunt bob and her deep blue eyes, she is beautiful.

"Welcome to the Circle House. Many treats await you. We have many rooms that will allow your stay to be whatever you need it to be. I am Scarlett. My job will be to show you all to a room each. Your host will see you at some point in your stay. But, for now, you have me. If there are no questions, follow me."

There are many questions floating in the heads of the group. Yet none of them can seem to open their mouths and ask. So they all just follow Scarlett into the very imposing building.

"OK all, this way."

Walking into the lobby, the light changes to a dull yellow. The interior of the place is not what is expected. The outside looks futuristic, yet the inside is not. The walls are painted in a cream colour, while the features are dark brown.

"Do not be confused. The lobby is neutral. The rooms are much more exciting."

Still, nobody can speak or ask any questions. It is as if they have been put on mute.

Scarlett then heads to a large wooden desk and gets some keys. There are six in total. Yet only four are in the group.

"Who wants the first choice?" Scarlett asks. Suddenly, everyone is then able to reply.

Julie steps forward before anyone else can, jumping up and down, demanding the first key. Scarlett looks at Julie with a smile and holds out the keys.

"Choose whichever key calls to you. It may seem strange, but you will see that the one you choose is going to be a perfect room for you."

Julie looks a little dubious, yet she takes a key. It has a bright blue keyring that looks like a gem of some kind.

"Oh, lovely. You have picked a great one. I shall just call one of my men to show you up, as this place can get confusing."

Suddenly, there is a tall bulking man standing by Julie with her bags already in his hand. He is very handsome; his hair is also black but short and neat. With dark blue eyes, that are like those of Scarlett's.

"Room Three, please."

Julie follows the man as he walks away while admiring his broad back, not taking in the place around her. It may cost her eventually.

Without much of a walk, they reach Julie's room. The door is blue, like the keyring, with a crustal number three in the centre. The handle and lock are also clear crystal. Julie then takes in her surroundings. There isn't another door on the floor, and she cannot remember going up any stairs or entering a lift. The man carrying her bags must be handsome if she cannot remember any of their walk to the room.

When Julie looks back to the door, it is open, and the man has taken her bags in already, so she walks in, and the door closes behind her.

Chapter Two
Room Three, Julie's Journey

Julie looks around her room. She is alone. The walls consist of four large screens.

"Welcome, Julie," an eery voice echoes through the small square space that should be her room.

"What is going on? Where are my things, and what is this room?"

"Oh, so many questions. You will have your answers soon enough. Now, look to the screens, and let's see what makes you who you are."

The room suddenly darkens then, and the walls start to show a film. There is a woman giving birth. Julie gasps. The woman is her mother.

"What is this?" she asks.

"Just watch, Julie. Your life events will appear. Let me get to know you better, so we can see where this journey will start."

The film changes. There is now a man standing over a cot. Julie is seeing everything as if from her own eyes. It is her dad.

"Hi, peanut, Mummy isn't well, sweetheart, so I must give you a bottle. Let's get you fed, shall we?"

Looking around, Julie recognises the house. It is when they lived in Devon. It is a little cottage that isn't far from a seaside town. It is surrounded by hills and fields, a beautiful place to grow up. Or so it would seem.

The screen changes again. Julie is sitting with her dad in the front garden of the cottage. She is probably about two here. Her mother is not in the picture. Julie is playing with a rattle and giggling happily. Her father is looking at her with love.

There is a loud crash then.

"Why are you showing me this?"

"Keep watching, Julie. We have a long way to go."

Looking back at the film, there is a lot of screaming and shouting.

Julie's mother has stormed into the garden with a broken bottle in her hands.

"Your bloody toys are everywhere, you little shit. You broke my bottle of vodka. It was nearly full!" Her mother screams at tiny Julie.

"Damn it, woman, she is a baby, and it isn't her fault that you are pissed again. Get a grip; this is not post-natal depression anymore, is it? You are using it as an excuse to get drunk. It is still morning, for fuck's sake." Julie's dad now screams at her and pulls the drunken woman away from now-crying Julie.

Everything changes again then. Julie is in school, six or seven years old here. Her blond hair is long and greasy, tied back with an elastic band. The clothes she wears are old and a little small. Those big green eyes of hers are shining with fear.

Several kids move out of her way as she walks through the school corridor, some holding their noses and others laughing.

"Stinks in here now," one boy yells. Julie just rushes to her class.

Again, the scene changes. There is now Julie's mother sitting in a flat of some kind. You can see that it is full of cigarette smoke. Butts scatters on the carpet, along with empty glass bottles. Julie is trying to clean up.

"Mum, the social is coming; please get up." A now ten-year-old begs her mum.

"Let them come. It would give me some peace. I should have let your dad take you like he wanted. You are pathetic just like him. Well, he can have you now. He'll get fed up with you as I have. You ruined my life. I was beautiful and fun before you came. I took you from him, didn't I? He left me, so I took you. His sad face was priceless. Such a pathetic man cries over a bitch like you."

As the screen changes again, Julie is sitting on the floor in tears.

"Why show this? Stop, please."

"Soon, there isn't much left to see."

On the screen is now a teenage Julie. She is clean now, with nice clothes. Her hair is cut into a neat bob. The sweet girl has now been replaced by a teen who likes to wear way too much make up and hangs out with boys who are so much older. They are all sitting in a park on some swings. The boys smoke weed, and Julie has joined them.

"Julie, what the hell are you doing?" Her dad yells as he storms towards her.

"What does it look like, Pops? Having fun with my friends. Are you proud of me, or are you going to drop me again?"

"This must stop. You know I didn't want to leave you. We have talked about this so many times. You are with me now. So please stop lashing out. Please don't turn into her."

"To late old man, now piss off, so I can have fun, just like she does."

"Julie, I love you. Please come back to me."

Again, the scene changes to her dad. He is older, with hair grey and wrinkles around his eyes. Julie must be about sixteen here.

She is making dinner and laughing with her father.

That is until the door smashes open and a group of young men storm in. Julie screams, and her dad yells at her to call the police, which she does.

"You took what is mine, old man. This bitch belongs to me, and I am taking her."

Julie's father then lunges at the leader, taking by surprise and plunging a kitchen knife into his stomach. The others see this, pull him off their friend and proceed to beat the father, while Julie screams at them to stop. Sirens are then heard, making the men run, leaving Julie to try and help her dad, who is bleeding badly on the floor.

"Daddy, I am so sorry that I bought those assholes into our lives. You mean everything to me. I love you so much."

"It is OK baby. I love you too. Just remember that you are not her; make me proud. Finish university and become something. Go and stay with your grandparents in London; they would love to see you. Your mother's parents would, too;

she didn't let them see you. Live a good life, my stunning daughter."

Julie has then watched the light die in his green eyes that looks so much like hers. Tears spill down her face that reminds her of the mother who has damaged her so much. Brushing her father's blond hair from his face, she kisses his head lightly as the police storms into their home.

Everything then turns black.

"Well, I guess that is it," the eery voice echoes again.

"Let us start your journey, young Julie. Those were just snippets of your twenty-one years on this earth. What comes next is up to you. Good luck, you'll need it."

"What the hell does that mean? Hello, creepy voice."

There is silence. A light then flashes revealing a completely different place in front of Julie's eyes.

Chapter Three

All around there is water; even the walls has vanished. Just never-ending, open water. Julie is terrified. She hates open water, especially what sits under the surface.

"What the hell is going on?" she yells into the open air.

"Choose," the same eery voice echoes around her.

"Choose what?"

As she stands there panicking, the man who has brought her to the room appears. He looks to be standing on the water.

"Julie, you will be asked a series of questions. If you answer correctly, a slab will rise, leading you to your next task."

"What am I doing here? Take me back to my friends. Now!"

The man just looks at her with his eyes that are void of emotion.

"I am your guide in a way. I cannot help you. I'm only here to direct you and make sure that you participate. You may not know my name or talk to me about anything other than the tasks ahead. I will not tell you anything else, so do not ask."

"This isn't right. I am supposed to be having the time of my life, not answering stupid questions."

The man just looks away and stares ahead. Julie looks down to see that she is standing on a slab. The water is clear, which lets her see what lies beneath. Her blood runs cold when a dark shape rises to the surface, showing a small shark, not just one; there are loads rising now. They are no ordinary sharks, about the size of a small dog. When one breaks the surface, Julie sees that it has very sharp teeth and a huge mouth that is covered in those jagged fangs.

"They may be small but will tear you apart in seconds."

"Why?"

He doesn't answer.

The booming voice then starts.

"Julie, you have not been the best person, have you? This will give you a chance to right the wrongs that brings you here. Or punish you for them. The choice is yours. The questions start now."

Julie is visibly shaking now.

"If you get the question right, a slab will rise. If you fail, a slab will fall, and maybe my hungry babies will have their fill. Then you must start over."

Questions

"Julie, is that your name? Easy first question."

"Yes! Please tell me what is going on. Let me leave."

A slab rises then, and the one she is standing on starts to shake making her step forward. Her pleas are ignored.

"Well done. Now this one is a little more difficult. Julie, did you love your mother?"

"What kind of a question is that? Of course, I did. Even if she was horrible, I still love her."

Another slab rises then.

"It seems that you did. Well, that is surprising."

The small sharks are now nudging the slab that Julie is on as if they are hoping she will fall off.

"Next question. Did you love your father?"

"Yes."

Another slab.

"Did you always?"

"No, not always. When he left me with her, I hated him."

And another.

"Looks like you are being honest. They do get tougher. Do not worry."

The man with Julie looks on. Still, no emotion shows on his handsome face. With each question that Julie answers, the closer she gets to the finish line. Or so she thinks. The sharks are getting hungry, and the path is leading to the centre of the vast space. There is nothing in sight, no end, and no beginning. After what seems like an eternity, the voice makes an offer.

"Answer me this and you shall have some food and a drink. When your father was killed, how did the men know where you lived? Why did they think you were being held by your father?"

Julie turns pale and looks down at her feet. The once confident woman is replaced with someone who has none.

"Answer me!" the voice bellows out now, and it is terrifying.

"I don't know." That is all she can get out. Then the slab falls away, and before Julie can get onto the previous one, the sharks are on her taking chunks out of her legs, until she pulls herself up. Blood is dripping onto the slab and into the water.

"Lie. It did not take long for them to start spilling from your mouth. Tell me, Julie. Did you cause your father's demise?"

Julie is stilled. Looking around her, she understands that there is no way out of this. Any answer she gave will condemn her. "What do you want from me?"

"Last chance, Julie. Answer the question."

"OK. Alright. I was young and stupid. I liked the attention. When they thought my father was keeping me from my man, they wanted to protect me. It felt good. I felt cared for. Adam, the man I was seeing, seemed so loving towards me. Until it turned to obsession. By then, I knew that what I let him believe was stupid. So I left him, and a note to say that we could not be together. Telling him nothing about my dad or that what he thought was wrong. That is on me. As for letting them know where we lived, that was not my doing. Maybe Adam followed us."

Everything has gone dark then, and the sky flashes. No longer a sky but a screen. A video is then played.

"Julie, half-truths are still lies. Watch the video. You had your chance."

Julie is watching as a scene plays out. Her skin is turning pale, and sweat is dripping down her forehead.

The screen shows Adam in his bed a phone pressed to his ear.

Julie listens as the conversation plays aloud.

"Baby, tell me where you are, and I will get you. He cannot stop you from leaving."

"Adam. I cannot tell you. He will know. But you can track me. When I come to you, take my phone and sort it. Then you will always know. I am yours always."

The screed goes black, and Julie is back to being surrounded by water. The creatures seem to be getting excited.

"I did not know. I was only fifteen when that happened. How was I supposed to remember? It was a stupid moment. A kid makes a stupid decision."

"A decision that cost your loving father his life. You need to pay, Julie. Your true self has been revealed. Manipulation and lies make up a false life. Prepare yourself. Punishment awaits."

Julie's screams echo as she feels the rock dropping from beneath her. She jumps over to the previous one; that too drops, as does the rest. All the creatures are around her doing nothing but watching and waiting.

"Julie, I hope this makes you see the error of your ways. There are so many more parts of your life that hurt others. This is only the start of what is to come. Have fun, my little friends."

At those words, the small shark-like fish head to Julie, slowly this time. Each takes a small bite, tormenting a screaming and terrified woman.

"I'm sorry. Please forgive me!"

Nothing. That was all there was. Just her screams as she was being eaten alive. Slowly and painfully.

Chapter Four

"Ahhhhhhhhhh!"

Julie wakes screaming. The pain is still fresh in her mind. Looking around, she sees that there is no vast space filled with water, just a lake not far away. The ground under her is soft and cool. Grass and mud are what is beneath her painful body. Trees surround where she sits with a path leading away from her. Julie studies herself. There are scars littering her body, red and angry-looking. Her own clothes are gone, and she is in a pair of white shorts and a red crop top, with red sandals on her feet.

Before her, there is a bag. In it, she finds food. Just an apple and water with a slice of bread. As she eats, the confusion hits hard. Was she dead?

"You are not dead, Julie. You do not deserve to have it easy yet. There are still so many things that you need to pay for."

It was the dark-haired man that took her to the room.

"Am I dreaming? Is this a nightmare that I cannot wake up from?"

"No."

"That is, it? Just no! Well, fuck you. I want my friends, and I want to go home. This is sick."

"Showing your true colours, Julie?"

"Stop saying my name like that. Let me go, you perv. Do you get turned on by seeing women get hurt?"

"Julie, I am just an observer. I do not interfere. This is your task. Take this path. Only your decisions and deeds can get you out of here. I would say good luck, but I do not like you, and I am hoping you fail. I have seen enough to think that you cannot be redeemed. Until we meet again, Julie."

Then he was gone.

"Asshole. I will get out of here. Do you hear me? You will pay for this! I will burn the Circle House to the ground. You and creepy voice will burn!"

The real Julie is certainly coming out now.

Her path is clear for her to start on this journey, yet she is hesitant to start. Thoughts of being torn apart flit through her mind. What else is awaiting her?

"Come on, woman, let's get this over with." Motivating herself, Julie walks towards the path, not looking back.

The Path

Three hours later, Julie is still at the start. No matter how fast she walks, the distance does not change. Giving up, that is what happens. Sitting on the hot path, Julie just looks at the bright blue sky.

"What am I supposed to do?"

There is that tree again, the one she was sleeping under. Another bag appears, with more food and a drink. She is so thirsty now. Getting up to retrieve her food, Julie spots a skinny dog who looks familiar lying where she had slept. He is panting in the heat and looks up to her. His tail is now wagging. In the bag, this time, there is a bacon sandwich, water, a small bowl of fruit and a carrot.

"What are you looking at?" she asks the friendly dog. "Do you have to show me the way?"

Looking at him again, Julie realises that he looks like the dog, which she has left at the side of the road by her. After going shopping one day, she has spotted a stray wandering around looking for food. Munching on a bacon sandwich, she has just looked at him. Wagging his tail looking at her hopefully, the dog thinks he is getting a bite of her food.

"This is mine, dog." That is all she said before getting in her car and driving off, leaving the poor boy with an empty stomach. Luckily, a sweet girl with big blue eyes and a bag full of food walks over to the dog.

"Hi, dog, I am Amy. Here you can eat my bacon. And I have water for you."

Julie sees this in the mirror of her car.

"Sucker." That is all she can say.

Remembering that day, Julie decides to do the right thing this time.

"Come here."

The sweet boy walks over to Julie, and she hands him the bacon while she eats the fruit and carrot with bread from her sandwich. She then gives the dog her empty bowl filled with half of the water. After the duo have had their fill, the dog runs down the path. Julie follows and realises that she is getting somewhere now. Realising that to go forward, she had to right a wrong, feeling guilty about the poor boy that she could have helped all those years ago.

Maybe there is a little good in her after all.

Walking along the road, there seems to be nothing but trees and fields. It is beautiful. Maybe this will not be as bad as Julie first thought. She can hope.

After what seemed like hours, a clearing appears ahead. The man is there waiting for her with a bag. As Julie approaches him, a small sneer appears on his handsome face, but it goes just as quickly that you would think it was not there at all.

"Julie, how is your journey going so far? No, do not answer that. I don't need to know as I can see it all."

She smiles at him and then sees the dog that helped her sitting by his side.

"This is Travis. He is a collie cross. I took him in when some nasty humans abandoned him. You showed him kindness this time, which gives you some points. Meaning I will talk to you about this once and advise you. The path ahead is long; do not deviate from it. There will be trials, so keep that in mind. It is going to get harder. Here are some supplies; take them and just keep going. Be patient."

After handing her the bag, Julie looks up to talk, but he has vanished again.

"Just great. Thank you, asswipe!" she shouts.

"Be patient, he says, after I have been torn apart, put back together and then walking for hours on end. Just peachy."

Julie sits in the clearing. Opening her bag, she sees that there are several bottles of water, some fruit and some kind of dried meat. There are also a couple of rolls.

After having some of the supplies, the very reluctant woman heads off to see how far she needs to go. Eager to get back and see her friends, she starts to run.

Half an hour of running, the path looks the same. There is another clearing, and Julie is tired, so she rests her feet has some water and falls asleep.

Waking up is hard with a sore body and aching feet. Yet Julie gets up and looks around. There is only one way forward. That is until she sees a girl in the distance coming towards her. Unlike Travis, there was no recognition.

When the girl gets closer, her features are clearly that of a child. Deep blue eyes and dark hair like the men here. Yet she is smiling and looks sweet, with deep dimples and pigtails.

"Hello, lady," she sweetly greets the haggard Julie.

"Um, hi. What are you doing here? Are you on a path as well?"

The girl giggles.

"No, silly. I live here. My name is Gracie. We have been watching, and I wanted to meet you."

"OK. Hi, Gracie. I guess you know who I am already. Can you tell me why I am here?"

"You are different. Most would be freaking out for a long time before starting. My brothers think you are cold. But I think you are strong and cool. Yes, I know who you are, Julie. But cannot tell you why you are here; answers come at the end. I can however help you get closer to it. If you come with me, there is a shortcut. It will take you closer to your goal and cut a lot of the journey. Otherwise, you will be walking for days. That will get boring for us, and I do not want you to break. I am rooting for you."

"I was told to be patient."

"Oh, yes. My brother hates you. We are supposed to be neutral, yet he is making things hard for you."

"That explains a lot actually."

Gracie smiles again and takes Julie's hand.

"You cannot let go. Only being with me can lead you out."

"OK, kid, let us do this. As soon as I am out, these people will pay. One more thing. Your brother said humans left his dog. Why did he reference humans that way? Are you not human?"

"Silly, lady, of course, we are. What else could we be? He likes to kid as does my eldest brother. Just ignore it."

"If you say so."

The duo walks a little further down the path. As they approach one of the trees, it opens to reveal a door. Gracie opens it to reveal the same path. Yet this one has no fields around it, just a wall.

"We are further along now. It has saved you days. Just walk through this door. Here is some more food, and I have put a treat in there for you. I also have some advice. Do not trust easily. What you see may not be the reality. What you feel may not really be there. Use your mind and feel with your gut. Truth can easily be made into a lie. Goodbye, lady. We shall not meet again."

Gracie then vanishes, leaving Julie really confused. Yet she walks through the door. Patience was never her strong suit. Anything for an easy way out.

Chapter Five

Stone walls everywhere. Regret hitting her hard. Without the journey, Julie does not know which way to go now.

"I told you to be patient, Julie. Now, you are stuck. Will you head out or end up back on the old path?"

There was that man again. Taunting her.

"Blame your sister. She convinced me to come this way."

"Blaming a child? You do not fail to surprise me. There was a choice, and you chose wrong. That is on you. Now find your own way. This path is far more difficult if you do not make the right choice. The path before would have given you what is needed to carry on. Good luck, you will definitely need it now."

"What does that mean? I was tricked! Don't just leave me here!"

Choices, we all have them. Yet some are not the right ones. Learning from the wrong ones is what life is made of. Hopefully, this wrong choice won't be the end for a very stubborn woman.

You may be wondering about the others. Well, they have chosen their own rooms, and soon enough, you know what they have gotten into. Right now, Julie's fate awaits.

No Way Out

"Come on, handsome, help a girl out," Julie calls out, but she gets no answer, not that she expected to. That sweet cherub really gets her. Remembering the words the girl said, Julie decides to try and get out.

Do not trust easily. What you see may not be the reality.

What you feel may not really be there.

Use your mind and feel with your gut. Truth can easily be made into a lie.

"Great, this is cryptic. I guess looking at the bag of treats might lift my spirits. Talking to myself is not doing much in the way of helping me."

Julie opens the bag that the kid has given her. There are some cakes, water, meat, cheese and bread and also a little fruit. Yet inside is also a box wrapped in sparkling silver paper and a note, which read:

I meant what I said, I am rooting for you. Sorry about the deceit. It wasn't personal. This will make up for it. I'm sure.

Julie is not optimistic about the present, and she hesitates. Will opening it be another trick? The kid says not to trust easily.

"Stuff it. What else can go wrong?"

Ripping open the gift, Julie is surprised at what is inside. There is a compass and a drawn map. It would have helped if she knows how to use it. Guess it is time to learn.

There was another note that said:

Use this to find your way to the start of this part of your Labyrinth, follow 'north'. When you find the start, use the map to get started. Do not detour, just follow the direction. Do not forget what I told you before I left. The compass is made to just point to the opening.

'Trust me'; go the 'direction' that I told you? 'Not' the 'SOUTH'.

Julie reads the letter several times. She wonders what is with all the quotation marks and a question mark at the end of told you? South is in capitals. Something clicks.

"I need to go south, not north." Looking at the compass, there are no directions, only an arrow now. Julie follows the paths although confused about why the need for north and south when it only shows one way on the compass. That is until she sees signposts with north and south on. It makes sense now. The signs would have sent her the wrong way. At the post, the compass arrow spins. Once Julie heads south, the compass sets itself right again.

Not knowing she is still being watched, the guard looks on, very angry at his little sister's antics. Julie should have been looking for days, and the tasks need to be accomplished. He decides to make sure nothing will be this easy going forward. With not being able to interfere, stalling her and distracting the vile woman will be all he can do.

Meanwhile, Julie follows the directions, hoping to get out of this hell. She walks for ages, seeing nothing but walls and dirt. The path is dusty and hot; heat radiates from the walls; her water is depleted. Sweat drips down her head and back.

"A little water would be nice!" Deciding to shout at nothing was getting her nowhere.

After what seemed like hours, Julie finally saw a door. It was a very old-looking wooden door with worn blue paint. At the front of it was a bottle of water and an apple.

"At last! Thank you, assholes!" Julie shouted before drinking the water and eating the apple with a ravenous hunger.

With her stomach satisfied and her thirst under control, she decides to try the door.

"Of course, it doesn't open."

While Julie is kicking the door, the guard stands behind her watching with amusement. "It will not open, Julie, until I do it."

This made her scream in surprise and turn to the man.

"You! What do you want?"

"You have three decisions to make: choose the right ones, and the door will open."

"Great, fine. Go for it."

The guard looks at Julie, taking his time. His hatred for the human is growing.

"Listen to my words. Answer with honesty only."

Julie just looks at him, waiting for the first choice.

"OK, you are dying a painful death. There is one friend who is healthy and happy with kids and a husband. One friend who is rich with everything except the ability to reproduce; then there is a friend who is also dying, but it will be quick and painless. You can choose to die as you are or swap with one of your friends. What do you choose?"

"That is easy. I would not swap."

"That is a lie. You only have two decisions left. Answer with honesty."

"Fine, the rich friend, she would deserve it."

"Too late. There is an extra punishment waiting for you. Your next decision. You are rich, but about to lose it all. You have three friends: one is poor but happy, with a family and a roof over their heads. The next is richer than you but very sick. Lastly is a friend who works hard and has a comfortable life. How would you handle the situation?"

"Weird question. Truthfully? I would not ask for help. I would swap lives with the richer friend, obviously."

"Yes, that is what I expected from you. Letting your friend suffer instead. There is no punishment as that was an honest answer."

"Yay. OK. What's next?"

The guard is annoyed. He doesn't want to let her continue yet. Still angry at his sister for helping. He hates the smug look on Julie's face.

"Last decision. This one decides if I let you in here or make you walk to the next door." This made Julie worry. She cannot walk in this heat much longer.

"You have a child. This child is innocent and sweet. You are a drunk, who only cares for herself. The money you get from having the child gets you what makes you high or intoxicated. The child's father wants her, but the money would stop. Do you allow the child a good life with the father and sort your life out? Do you change your ways and give the child a mother she deserves, or do you tell her that she is unwanted by her father to keep getting your money?"

"That is not fair. How can I answer? My mother's decisions are not mine."

"But this is what you would do. The greed is in both of you. Would you make the same choice that your mother made?"

"No. I would not. None of these choices are what I would do. If I were a drunk and a junkie, there would be no child. I may be greedy, but my child would not be a porn. Not like I was. I would never follow in her footsteps."

"Not one of the choices, but it is the truth. So you can pass. Remember there is a punishment waiting. Goodbye, until next time."

The door opens then, and the guard vanishes. Julie takes hesitant steps through the door. When she is in the room, the door slams shut.

Julie turns, trying to get back out after seeing what awaits her.

Chapter Six

The Room

"Let me out! I cannot be in here with that. Please!" Julie begs, but there is nobody to help her.

The room holds a sofa, table and a TV. On the dirty carpet, there is a soft toy, a gun, a metal bat and a huge hammer. There are also several empty bottles, needles and tin foil pieces.

On the sofa sits a woman with greasy hair falling over her glazed eyes. Her skin is pale, and her body is thin. Her once beautiful face is now sunken and sweaty with sores and dry thin lips.

"Mother?" Julie can do nothing but stare, frozen in place.

The woman looks up; her face suddenly turns furious. Her eyes look right at Julie. Blood starts to pour from her eyes dripping onto the white dressing gown that covers her thin frame.

"You will pay for everything." That is all that the woman is saying before she lunges at Julie.

Her body, although thin, is strong. Knocking Julie to the floor. Her dirty nails dig into Julie's flesh as she claws at her with anger, while the younger woman tries the shield herself.

Without thinking, Julie grabs the nearest thing on the floor. It is the gun, which happens to be loaded.

Her face is covered in blood. Scratches cover her now. The older woman does not stop. She is relentless. Julie has no choice but to pull the trigger.

Everything stops; the silence is deafening. Standing up on shaking legs, Julie looks down at her mother's body. There is blood everywhere. As Julie looks closer, the body is no longer her mother but her father. He is lying dead at her feet.

"No! What is this?"

Looking towards the sofa again, her mother is back.

"Is this my punishment? Please stop!"

Her mother screams again and starts to run towards Julie. This time, she dodges her mother and falls over her dad's body. His blood covers her hands and knees. The claw marks have gone now. Only scars remain, amongst the others on her body.

Grabbing the bat now, Julie swings it and hits her screaming mother. The woman falls with blood pouring from her head, landing on the male.

Again, the body is no longer her mother. Duke is now lying there dead, the man she thought was the love of her life and saviour all those years ago.

This continues. Each time Julie strikes her mother down, the body is someone from her past. Friends from college and childhood friends. The room is almost full of bodies and blood.

"Please stop this!" she begs.

Again, her mother appears before her. Rage is still in her eyes. Julie looks around. Every weapon has been used, and none have stopped this. All that remains is the cuddly toy.

"What are you trying to make me do? You will not break me!"

Julie picks up the bear. It is one from her childhood when she has love from the person in front of her.

Julie is charged again. This time instead of hitting her mother, Julie pulls the raging woman into a tight embrace, showing love instead of violence.

"It is OK, Mum. I am here. Let it all out. I love you still after everything."

The raging stops. The screaming no longer echoes through the room. All the bodies vanish, including the replica of her mother.

Julie is standing alone now. The room is clear of everything except a door. However, she does not move terrified of what is next. Has she already had the punishment?

Nothing could be worse than this room, right?

"I cannot do this anymore. Please let me go home. I have learnt so much. Can you not see that? I will be nicer to dogs. I will care instead of lashing out. You want me to be honest. Well, I will. Tell me what I must do."

"You must finish. It is that simple." The guard appears and berates her again.

"Go through the door, Julie. Food and water await. There may even be time to sleep, or not."

Julie does not say a word and only walks up to the door. It is also blue, but it is made of thick frosted glass. Reaching for a blue crystal handle, she starts to sweat and shake.

"Get a grip. This is not that hard. You are strong. Turn the knob," which she does.

Once through the door, there is nothing but dark blue light. The room looks like it is also made of blue frosted glass;

the light is coming from outside. The whole place looks like a dome. No doors, no windows. The entrance has disappeared, and so has the guard.

Julie sits on the cold floor, not knowing what else to do. As promised a water bottle appears along with a bag of crackers, cheese, some grapes, and an apple.

When the food and water have been consumed, a mattress appears on the floor. It is a blow-up single that is made of clear blue plastic. Julie realising how tired she is crawls over to it and falls asleep instantly, only to be woken up by loud banging that is coming from outside of the dome. When it stops, she tries to get back to sleep. When her eyes close, the banging starts up again.

"Seriously? I am exhausted!"

This goes on for a long time, with only a few minutes of sleep between bangs. There is only one thing Julie can do now. That is to get up and find a way out.

Forcing herself up, the searching begins.

Chapter Seven

The Search

This room is not what it seems. There is something not quite right about it. Was this place supposed to be on Julie's path? Can she get out of this with her sanity intact? It is already being affected.

Where is the exit? Where is the sound coming from?

Julie walks around the structure, feeling every surface, but it was smooth everywhere. The banging only occurs when she tries to rest.

"How is this helping anyone? Let me out!"

As she screams at the dome, banging the surface, a light flickers behind the glass. Then a crack forms where Julie placed her hand, continuing to strike the glass with harder hits and kicks. The dome finally comes down around her, shards of glass cutting into the delicate flesh of her face and arms. Bright light surrounds Julie blinding her. With the dome crumbling beneath her, Julie has no idea what to do. There is no path, nothing to hold on to. The glass under her feet is all that is holding her up starts to crack now.

"What have I done? Why am I so stupid?" Berating herself for using force, Julie accepts her fate; she steps off the glass into the light.

Falling into an abyss, there is nothing but light. All the blue has gone. Julie realises that she is floating rather than falling now. Pictures of her life flash in front of her. There are good and bad amongst the many clips of her. One stands out. A small girl with glasses and dark hair is in the picture. Her nose is bloody, and bruises are over her tiny face. Julie remembers her. Aubry was sweet and funny, always trying to make friends. She is the type of girl that everyone liked, all except Julie.

Break time has come, and the kids all rush out to the climbing frames. Aubry is extra excited. She holds invitations to her upcoming party, which is being held at the community centre, with loads of exciting things happening. Aubry's parents are not rich, but they have saved to give her a party to remember.

Julie stares at the small girl as she runs around giving each child an envelope.

Then Aubry runs up to Julie smiling.

"Here you are, Julie. I hope you can come. Please don't worry about a present or anything, just you being there will be enough. It is going to be sooooo much fun."

"You think I cannot afford a present?"

"No, of course not. It is just I only need my friends. You are my friend."

Julie has so much hate then for the sweet girl in front of her with her perfect parents and a stupid smile always on her stupid face. Without a second thought, Julie hits Aubry in the face and continues to hit her. Kids run over trying to get Julie away from Aubry.

"We are not friends! I hate you and your stupid happy face!"

Memories then flood the present Julie. All the time she hurt people out of jealousy. More pictures flash in front of her. Guilt hits her hard.

"I am sorry. OK! I was a kid."

More images, some as an adult. The same things. Hurting people out of jealousy.

Julie realises then that all she has to do is live. Instead of looking at others' lives, she can have just enjoyed her own. The friends are there for her and a wonderful father who loves her.

Looking down Julie sees another dome. It is not really a dome when you look at it. The shape looks like a brain. A brain made of thick frosted glass. The banging Julie realises is memories hitting the glass from the outside. Regrets stopping her from resting. Things that never really bothered her in life.

Falling fast now, she starts to panic. The glass structure is getting closer. There is nothing that can stop the impact. Julie is going to hit it.

Once she reaches the big blue brain, instead of hitting it, Julie falls straight through it and lands on a bed. Another plastic blow-up bed. Tiredness hits, and sleep takes over. This time there is no banging.

The guard appears then and leaves supplies by the bed. He looks at the sleeping woman.

"Rest while you can. There is so much more you have to suffer for."

Leaving Julie to sleep, the guard vanishes again.

Waking with a yawn, Julie looks around her. The blue has gone now, and in the place of it is another field and path. Finding the food and water, she quickly replenishes her energy. Standing up and stretching while taking in her surroundings, Julie notices that the path is now made of blue brick. On closer inspection, it is made up of glass bricks. If she weren't so broken, it would look pretty.

Knowing now that all she can do is walk down the path. Follow it and see what is next.

So Julie walks, not wanting to wait for the next obstacle. The journey takes its toll on her physically and mentally.

Her journey is almost complete, but this is not going to be easy for her. An ending isn't guaranteed. Will she earn her way out?

Chapter Eight

The Blue Path

The path ahead is a long one, unlike the others this one can lead straight to Julie's demise or redemption. There will be no second chances, no redos or help from anyone. This will be all her.

This place is packed with dangers. As Julie walks along, she spots a man. He has his back to her and has something in his hand. Is this another test? Will Julie leave the path to assist the man?

"Hello, do you need help?"

No answer, but the man starts to turn around at hearing her shouting. Julie then screams. His face is twisted; like a melted candle his skin drips on the black shirt that he is wearing. He is holding what looks to be flowers. Yet they are dead and falling apart. This being looks familiar to Julie. His green eyes are striking, even though they are halfway down his face.

He starts to walk towards her with slow steps. His hands now drips like his face as he reaches for her.

Julie cannot move, frozen in place by fear.

"Move, Julie, come on! Move your feet!" Her pep talks not working. She just stands there and stares at the thing coming for her.

As he gets near, Julie starts to see that there is something familiar about him. Those eyes and clothes, maybe the flowers too. The realisation hits then. She has dated him; this thing looks like Greg. He is handsome, rich and heading for greatness. They have dated for a year until he has moved away to study. Greg is shallow and only interested in looks. He only cares about himself, which suits Julie, as she is the same at the time.

"Greg? Is that you?"

The man says nothing. He just keeps walking towards her. The skin on his body now drips red, and his eyes and features are now just a mess of flesh and blood. The dark jeans he wears fall from him and pools to the floor. Muscle and fat now slipping off his bones. His shirt clings to bones and blood. Expensive Italian shoes holds in the remains of Greg's feet.

"What is the lesson here?"

There is no answer. Just silence, which is only broken by small groans and slopping sounds as more flesh falls. He reaches to Julie again, holding out the dead flowers that are now covered in blood.

"I get it now. Would I want someone if they are not perfect or if they lost their looks? Is that it?"

What Julie did not realise is that this is not a test. This part of the journey is not about that. It is so much more.

With a shaking hand and tears falling, she reaches her hand out and takes the flowers just as Greg collapses in a pile of bones, skin, blood and body parts.

In the mess, there is a bright blue glass heart. Reaching down, Julie picks it up, ignoring the gore. Inside the heart, she can see what looks like a key. To get it, the heart needed to be broken. Without a second thought, it is thrown to the floor and smashed, revealing a silver key. The flowers then turn into a bottle of water, which Julie really needs.

"This place is so weird. How long is this path? Can anyone answer me?"

Again, she gets no reply.

Turning to look back at the path, Julie begins to walk again, as if nothing has happened. This woman is hard to break. She does not care much for anything. That will change. The journey is not over yet.

The path comes to a crossroad. There is a blue path that heads to the left, a black which heads straight and a silver path to the right. No signposts or hints this time.

Guessing that silver is the best way because of the key, Julie heads in that direction.

A little way down, she realises that the path is getting hot. The sun above is heating the metal.

All Julie can do is run. Her soles melt if she stands for too long. In the distance, there are shadows along the path, which makes Julie run harder and faster trying to get to them.

The effort is useless as she sees what the shadows are. They are corpses. Burnt and smoking bodies, which are stuck to the metal path. Each has a silver key that is held tight in the crusty fingers of the decaying hands.

Feeling sick at the sight, Julie starts to run again, not wanting the same fate to befall her.

"Help me, please?" Julie hears a voice. It is faint.

Turning around, she sees that one of the burning bodies still has its eyes, and they are looking at Julie, pleading.

"I guess you need help, and then my task will be done. Great. OK, smokey, let me do what I can." Hoping from one foot to the other, so as not to melt her shoes completely, Julie takes in the maybe female before her. Deciding that there is not much she can do. The bottle of water in her hand has only a little bit left in it.

"OK, drink this." Putting the bottle to the charred lips of the person, Julie pours the remaining water into the hot mouth.

Instantly, the mouth turns back into pink lips, and the body takes the form of a striking woman, with dark red hair and hazel eyes.

"We are all here for a reason. I am Clair, a psychopath and a mad woman. This place will not let me go. I am a lost cause you see. There is nothing I can do to help you. If there was, then we would not be here. But thank you for the water. That gives me a little more time before I burn again. Small relief from the pain and this horrid path. Bring back the water I say."

"Anyway, this is not getting me anywhere. My shoes are long gone. There is one piece of advice that will help a little. The key is useless. You helped me, so I will not hurt you or take your shoes this time. Maybe when we meet again. They lied to you; this path isn't unique; otherwise, little old me wouldn't be here. Would I? Unless I am a test. Confusing, isn't it?"

"I lost my mind ages ago, probably why they won't let me leave. You see nothing should get to me, with being psychotic and all, so why am I affected? These people are good. Believe it or not. It is up to you."

After all that, Clair runs away.

"Well, that was helpful."

Going over what the woman said, Julie remembers what the girl told her way back. It suddenly becomes clear. Clair is lying. She is psychotic and mad after all. But what was she lying about? Deciding to ignore it all and just run.

And run she does. For a very long time. There is nowhere to go; if she steps off the path, it will just put you back on it. Forward is the only viable option. There are several more bodies, all smoking and smelling bad. Burnt hair and nails are pungent in the air now, as the corpses increase.

Finally, there is something different, no more silver; the path ahead turns into a blue path again.

"Typical, I should have stayed on the blue. Stupid woman."

The fields return, and there is water. No food, though.

Julie collapses on the grass by the blue path. Her energy depletes. The water is gone in an instant. Sleep takes over her then, which is dangerous in this place. Yet her body does not seem to get the message.

Will Julie wake? If she does, will everything be as it should be?

Chapter Nine

Awake?

"OK, I am up. Turn off the alarm already."

Julie opens her eyes then and realises that it is not an alarm that is going off, but something much worse.

All around her are corpses again, but they are screeching, walking and grabbing at her. Reaching out, they are trying to take her key.

It confuses her, as they all have their own.

"Get off me!"

Reaching, grabbing and screeching. Their blisters drip onto Julie's clothes.

Nothing will stop them. Each body has a key welded into the fingers that are holding it. Some have holes where eyes used to be; others have white orbs or red dripping balls.

Crawling away from them, Julie tries to get back on the path. It is futile. They will not let her go.

Looking at them, she realises that the keys they hold are not whole keys; they have melted and are part of the hand that is holding it. None of them would work. That is why they want hers so badly.

Julie is getting desperate now. She starts to kick and push with her feet. Never let the key go.

Someone grabs her hand and pulls her to the path. Looking up, she sees Clair.

"You helped me?" Julie asks her, with a shocked expression.

"An eye for an eye. But I do want something from you for this."

"You will not have my key, Clair."

"The key you hold is useless. The key you hold will not work. That is not what I need from you. Just your shoes, so I can carry on. Remember, they are lying to you, and the key you hold is useless."

"You have told me that already. Oh, I see. You are 'not' helping me. My shoes are the least I can give you. Here." Julie removes her shoes and hands them to Clair. "Clair, why can't the corpses walk on the blue path, but you can?"

The bodies are all standing at the side of the path. Still screeching and trying to reach out, but not touching the blue path.

"They are lost, and there is nothing left of the people they were. This path can only hold those that are still functioning. I could not walk it until you revived me. I am going now. Maybe after helping, they will let me out. Hopefully, I can run as far as you did."

Before another word can be uttered, Clair has run off again, leaving Julie to stare at the things wanting her key. More of them have appeared, and these are more skeletal than the others.

Taking in her appearance, she realises that there are scratches all over her body now. Her dress is ripped, and some parts are shredded. More scars to add to her body.

Grabbing part of the torn dress, Julie pulls it, tearing off a strip. She then attaches it to the key and ties it around her wrist.

"Should be safer there, I think. Talking to yourself, Jules. You are going insane now, aren't you?"

There is nothing else to do but walk now. With hunger hitting and her feet sore, Julie just carries on, keeping an eye on the corpses that are following alongside her.

"You are so creepy; leave me alone! Stop following me; you are not getting my key."

But follow her they do. Knowing something that Julie does not, they will not leave her side.

Hours pass by, and the path is not going anywhere. Thirst is hitting Julie hard now, and rest is desperately needed.

In the distance, there is a blue box. It is clear blue glass, so when Julie gets closer, she sees that there is water and food in it. However, the box is situated by a tree in a field. This is what they were waiting for. Julie needs to leave the path; her supplies are waiting. Does she leave the safety of the path or carry on without the water and food she desperately needs?

Knowing she has no choice, Julie tries to work out a plan in her head to get the box and keep the key.

Nothing catches Julie's eye. The bodies are all waiting for her to cross, so they can get what they want.

An idea forms. Clair's words come back to her.

The key you hold is useless, the key you hold will not work.

"The key I hold? Of course! Way to go, Clair."

Julie unties the key from her wrist and then places it on the blue path, as far away from the bodies as possible. She walks a little further, noticing that the corpses do not follow. They will not let the key out of their sight.

Running with all she has left, Julie heads towards the box. Lifting the lid and pulling out the water bottle and bag of food.

"Yes! I win you walking body bags."

Running back to the path, Julie sits and enjoys her food, which consists of cheese sandwiches and fruit. There is a protein bar also, which she decides to save, along with half the water.

The key still sits where she left it. Picking it up and tying it to her wrist again, Julie starts walking with a smile on her face.

Oh, that will change soon enough. Let the last bit of fun begin.

Chapter Ten

The Last Leg

Well, poor Julie has had it rough, and she has a huge surprise when the journey ends. But that will come eventually. Will it be good? Maybe, or not. Only one way to find out.

The blue path just keeps going. More bodies try to follow. Some are starting to fall apart; others are decaying a lot but standing firm. None of them want to give up.

With all the bodies, however, Julie does not get any unwelcome melting visitors. There are no diversions or crossroads. Her food has all gone, and there is only a drop of water left. She cannot see if there are any boxes, as the corpses have multiplied so much that it is like a thick wall of bodies that don't end. Walking on is the only option again.

With Julie losing hope and more of her sanity, she is tempted just to throw the key into the mass and try to find food. That would be very stupid of her though. Instead, she looks into the distance; there in front of her are two doors not too far away. Running now to get there and leave this weird place.

The doors are both wooden. One black; the other blue. Julie takes her key and views the holes. The key will fit both by the look of it. So there is a choice.

"I cannot take any more blue."

"That is your choice, Julie." The guard is back.

"Oh, it is you. Hiding away, were you?"

"I only watch and give questions occasionally. You know this. Now, this is just a choice. One door leads to salvation, and the other leads to your demise. Only gut instincts shall lead you. Fate will give what is deserved. I shall not see you again. This is where we part. It has not been a pleasure. Goodbye."

"Bye then." Julie was left alone to decide her fate.

"Gut instincts. OK, I can do this."

Julie gets a feel for the doors. Touching each one in turn. Both feel the same to her. She cannot get rid of the feeling that the blue door is not the one she wants, as all she has seen is blue, and it has not been good.

"OK, I have decided. That black door looks so much better to me, and the path I did not try was black. So that is the one. Come on, Julie, open the door."

And that is what she does. The door opens wide, and through she goes.

Darkness surrounds her. A light comes on, and Julie is back in the room that started all of this.

"Hello again, Julie."

That creepy voice echoes through the room.

"You are here until your friends finish their journeys. Your fate is sealed and will be delivered eventually. Because of the shortcut, you arrived too early. So sleep or sit and watch your life again. The choice is yours."

"You are joking? I must wait. No! This is so unfair! I did all that was asked. I was tricked into the shortcut. Just let me go. You dick. This is my life, and I want to leave."

"I thought that you would have learnt patience by now, young Julie. Oh, wait, you like shortcuts. Do not think I am a nice person just because I am polite. Do not test me, woman! This is your only chance. Now sleep or do not. Goodbye for now."

"I hate you. Fine, I will sleep. Bye."

And that is what she did until she was summoned for the results.

Chapter Eleven
Room Nine, Duke's Story

After Julie leaves us, the others eagerly await their turn.

They really should not.

The one who is called Duke steps forward to retrieve his key. A stunning female steps forward with his suitcase while he decides. She has dark hair like the male before her and the same striking blue eyes. Duke, being a gentleman, tries to take his case from her.

"You don't have to take my case, beautiful. I can take it myself." Winking at her in the process.

"Choose your key, please," Scarlett firmly tells him. The beautiful woman holding the bag only smiles at Duke and gives him a sneaky wink.

With a big grin, the guest chooses his key. He looks at them all, yet one stands out. It is bright orange, with a matt texture, reminding him of a happy day in his childhood, painting with his friends at school. This colour was always his go-to for finger painting.

"This one. It called to me."

"Good choice." Scarlett attests. "This lovely lady will show you the way."

Duke turns, giving the key to the lovely lady, while he grabs his case before she can retrieve it.

"I've got this. Please lead the way."

Shaking her head, she walks in the opposite direction that Julie went. Yet Duke didn't mind this, funny when he tells her all the time how right for each other they are. How wrong he is.

Duke is let down a hallway. The doors are all dark silver and grey, with a crystal knob. None of them have numbers.

Without questioning, he continues to follow. Blindly trusting the beauty before him.

Finally, they reach a door with the number nine on it, in the same orange as the key. Duke looks back, and he realises that the others cannot be heard. He did not think they walked that far.

Looking back to his door, he sees that it is open, and the lovely lady has disappeared with his case, Duke walks to his door. Assuming that she went into the room he steps inside, the door closes behind him.

"Hello, beautiful. Where did you go?"

The room is dark. Finding a light switch, Duke lights up the room. It is a decent room, decorated in grey and orange, with a silver framed bed in the centre. A cute little grey draws each side of it. His suitcase is situated by the door. The bed has very soft grey covers, with orange sheets and pillowcases to match the bedding.

Sitting on the bed, Duke takes a deep breath and lies back. That is when the fun starts.

All the lights go out, leaving the room in complete darkness.

Duke is terrified.

"Hello? Please put the lights back on," he shouts at nobody in particular.

"Hello, Duke," a male voice echoes through the room.

"Lights, please. I cannot take the darkness."

A small orange glow appears by the bed.

"There you go, Duke. We cannot have you freaking out just yet. Now please listen to me before interrupting and save all your questions for later."

"OK, go ahead, and thank you for the light."

"Duke, you are about to start a journey. One that will show who you really are. This confident facade to have, it needs to be tested. Soon, I will show you snippets of what I have seen. Then your journey will begin. Now, ask me the questions you have burning in your mind."

"I am OK. I don't want to ask anything of you. I'm sure it will come together, and I'll figure it out."

"Nothing? Not who I am, what this is or what's going on?"

"I'm sure you will tell me eventually."

"That I will, Duke. Now sit back and enjoy."

The room lights up then as picture forms. Duke's life starts to play out before him.

This man is a curious one. His insides do match the man he lets others see. I am looking forward to this one.

Chapter Twelve

Duke's Past

As Duke looks up, the first thing he sees is his mum. She is in pain in the back of a car; a man is there with her yelling for her to push. It is Duke's birth.

There is blood everywhere. The man does not help her; he just freaks out and runs away, leaving his mother alone.

As she screams for help, a homeless woman walks past and sees her. Instantly, she helps.

"Do not worry, dear, I was a nurse. I am not very clean I am afraid, but you need help now. It cannot wait. Your child is breached, and you are bleeding out. Stay with me and do what I say. OK?"

The picture changes then. Duke's mother is lying in a hospital bed, pale and sleeping. A man walks by and looks at her. He is a porter for the hospital. Duke's face morphs when seeing the man. It is now one of fear and hatred.

Changing again, there is now a little boy of two, playing with blocks, while his mother looks on, lovingly.

"That's it, baby; build us a home. You are so smart."

The love is undeniable. Smiling happily, both play. Unaware that they are being watched, the man from the hospital looks on. Taking everything in.

Again, the film skips to a future scene. The boy is now four. He is playing with a small truck in the garden. His mother is making dinner. The man is watching the boy.

"Dad, why is Mummy cooking so late? Why do we have to have your food? Can I have spaghetti? Mum makes good spaghetti. I do not like pies."

The man moves fast. He hits the boy hard in the hip.

"No more questions, boy. For each question, you get a hit. Keep going, and it will be much worse. Tell your mum I will hit her twice as hard as you. And she will leave."

"OK."

The videos keep playing. Each time shows the man hurting the boy. Making excuses for the bruises that he fights with friends and they get rough. Or he falls climbing some trees. Football is extra hard this time. Always excuses. Duke has a place that he is put in also. It is a metal shed, with no windows. No matter the weather, Duke is put in it. Only when his mother goes to her little job waiting tables at a local café. The man loves to hear the screams when it gets too hot or freezing.

Duke's mum excepts them all despite the doubt. He treats her well, pays the bills and makes sure they want for nothing. He even lets her spend the earnings she makes on herself and Duke.

Looking at the screen, Duke has tears in his eyes, but he doesn't let them fall.

The pictures change to a happy time. Children are playing in a classroom and painting with their fingers.

"I want the orange, please. It is bright and happy. It chases away the dark, like the sun does," young Duke asks the lady handing out colours.

All the children work together and take some lovely pictures. Duke smiles wide at his friends. They have more paint on themselves than on the canvas.

More of the film plays out. Duke's mum becomes more oblivious to the problems. She is married to a man now. The once bubbly woman has turned into a shell of herself. The love she has for her son is still strong. It is just her light that has gone.

Light bruises showing along her arms now. Once they were married, the abuse starts with Duke's mum. The films show how he will get angry when Duke speaks, raising his fists and raining fury down on her instead, the hits to Duke doesn't seem to get the effect he wanted anymore, so he will make Duke watch him hit the woman.

The abuse gets worse as Duke ages. His mother is no longer able to work. She has no friends, and her husband makes sure to drive them away. Duke is sent away to college not knowing that it will destroy what was left of his mother. At sixteen, all that mattered is leaving the place he is supposed to feel safe.

At eighteen, college is going great. Although Duke is haunted by the past, his life is full of laughter and friends. That is until his mother is supposed to visit him.

It is a Friday night; everyone is out at a party. As expected, Duke's mother has not turned up that morning. They have planned to go into town and have food, maybe shop a little. Duke wants to spoil his mum with the money he gets from working part-time at a local sports shop. He is so excited; it has been two years of mostly chatting on the phone with the occasional trip to see her. Each time her husband is not at home. Not being there, Duke hoped that his mother would have been safe. After all, his mum is only beaten because of him.

That is not the case. The pictures show what Duke has not see at the time. His mother is dragged into a room with several men. The scene in the room is not shown, but the screams say everything. Her supposed husband is standing by the door counting a wad of twenty-pound notes.

Then there is silence.

Duke remembers a call he got at the party. His mother is found, raped and strangled. She has been lying in a field; a jogger has found the body. It has been there just one night. He knows whose fault it is, but there is no evidence to connect the death to the man he used to call Dad.

That night changes Duke even more. He shuts off any emotions, turning into the cocky and confident man he is today. All fake of course.

The film showing bits of the past stops then. Duke has tears in his eyes and down his face.

"That was an interesting past, Duke. We are not finished yet. Take a breath, and I will carry on."

Duke is just silent.

When the room shows the next video, it is of a young girl. She is about eighteen, with dark hair that is cut into a long bob that hides her big innocent brown eyes. Duke is with her in a hotel room; he is twenty. After treating her like a queen, she gives him what he wants without a second thought.

Duke does not even look at her after. He just gets up and leaves the poor girl naked on the bed.

This is a regular occurrence. Duke always leaves the poor women.

The confidence he has comes from drugs and alcohol, numbing his past and turning him into a robot.

That is until Julie has come into his life. He wants her, but she keeps him wanting.

They meet at a party and become fast friends when she calls him out for his womanising ways. Both broken and in need of someone.

At the party, Amy and Benny are also in attendance, but that is another story.

Duke, even though wanting Julie, continues to break hearts. The drugs are stopped, but the drink hasn't. Sex and alcohol still numb the pain from his past.

The scene changes again, and Duke is standing over the broken body of a man. His stepdad's limp body was covered in blood and stab wounds amongst other injuries. Duke is numb. He finds other victims of that horrible man. All of them come together and take things into their own hands.

Finding the asshole in a bar, they lure him outside. Julie is the one who gets him out, using her beauty. Once he is outside, she knees him between the legs. The others grab him and gag the murderer. Then after knocking him out, they drag him off to finish the job.

Taking their time to beat him, the group gets the revenge they wanted. After the last blow that has killed him, Duke feels nothing. Everyone has left, but he could not. The sight in front of him accomplishes nothing. He is still broken, except now he is a murderer also. He may not have landed the final hit, but he is part of it all.

The scene goes dark again.

"There is nothing else that needs to be seen now. Your journey will start. Follow your guide. She will show you the way."

Duke says nothing. He just gets off the bed and stands up. The room then changes before his eyes. He is in a silver room, bright orange lava dripping from the ceiling and landing in a pool on the floor. The beautiful woman who showed him to the room is then by his side.

"Let us get this started, shall we?" she states.

Chapter Thirteen

Duke's Path Starts

Looking around and taking everything in, Duke has so many questions. But he will never ask them. His guide decides that she should just tell him what he needs to know.

"Duke, I am your guide and guard. You cannot know my name. This path of yours will have many obstacles. Each you need to accomplish to get to your destination. Not everyone gets to the end, but you need to try. This room is just for you."

Duke remembers what he has done. There is a foundry that Duke uses to dispose of the body. It is still hot from workers not long left. The lava reminds him of that night. "You will have questions, and you need to answer honestly. Every fail has consequences."

Duke just nods. This man is not conveying the confidence he had earlier.

"OK, let us start then."

Again, just a nod.

"Right, first question. This one is easy. It will just give you an idea. What is your favourite food?"

"I do not have one now. It was spaghetti bolognaise that Mum used to make. It was rare we had it, so I loved it."

"Oh, more complicated than I thought. OK, so you see the lava is depleting. Well, there is a door at the bottom of the pool. We need to get you there. Fail and it fills up; the more you fail, the faster it fills. It will not stop, and you will burn. The heat will get stifling. Are you ready for this, Duke?"

"Bring it on, beautiful." The confidence reappears suddenly. Duke's coping mechanism rears its head.

The room is getting so hot; it is making thinking hard.

"OK, next question. Do you hate your mother for not leaving that man?"

"Yes, what is next?"

"Strait to the point I see. Do you forgive her?"

"I don't know. I want to."

"This is going to be a quick round, Duke. I guess honesty is not a problem for you?"

"Nope, why lie? It gets you nowhere."

"Right, a hard one then, I guess. Do you feel any guilt for hurting all those women? Breaking their hearts and spirits to ease your own insecurities."

"I feel nothing. Maybe a little bad after seeing it, but it was fun for both parties each time. I did kind of lead them to believe I wanted more. That I regret."

"Oh, you are lying. The guilt is eating you up. You wanted a connection, but fear took over. You are not as numb as you try to appear. Interesting."

The lava rises then, and some spits out towards Duke, burning his arm. It is weird; each piece that spits out looks like a finger, and they crawl like worms.

"That is creepy. What the hell are those?" Duke asks.

"You'll see. I am not spoiling the surprise."

The room starts to feel small, like the side are moving in. The pool is not as full, but it is just as hot. Duke tries to see what is mixed with the flaming liquid. It looks to him like moving body parts. Bits are trying to crawl out. The blood has mixed with the yellow lava, making it the bright orange that it is. Not burning away, just mixing, like paints. The pieces are similar to living organisms, swimming in the burning hot liquid. White hot sparks also spit out, making dints in the silver floor that Duke is standing on. It is beautiful but deadly.

"Any questions in that head or yours? There must be some."

"No, I am good. Just give me another question, please. Let us get this over with."

"OK, but I will give you a little hint. Be honest with yourself."

Duke doesn't know what to do with that. He has hidden feelings for so long and lied to himself for just as long.

"Next question then. If you had slept with Julie, would you have run away after that?"

"Who knows? I honestly don't know the answer to that. There is a possibility."

"That is too vague. I need more."

"Fine. I would not have wanted to, but running is what I do. So, yes, I probably would have and then hated myself for it."

"Better. That is the honesty I am looking for. Now, the next question needs to come from you. You can ask anything about this room."

"No, I can't do that. Just raise the lava."

"Not an option. I can stand here all day. You must ask. The lava has reduced a little from your honesty. If you ask me a question, you will be able to go. The next task awaits a nice cold bottle of water. Only good can come from you asking."

Duke is stuck. His mind is set. Questions cause others pain. He only asks them when it is his friends. He does not know this woman.

Just because she is stunning does not mean that she can be trusted.

Thinking over his options, Duke decides that it is worth the risk this time.

"OK, right. What are those things crawling in the pit?"

"I knew you were curious about that. See, it wasn't so bad. That is living human flesh. It wants to merge with a host, burning flesh in the process. Don't worry the person who lives in the lava was very bad. Burnt beyond pain. It feels nothing. Do not show pity. It will not give you any."

"That is sick. Nobody deserves to be in that state."

"There are no thoughts or feelings not, only the need to cling on to a living host."

"Still, I don't like it."

"No, I suppose you don't suppose you do. We can leave now; look the door is clear. You aced this part. From now on, I cannot assist you. I've already done more than I should. But your story calls to me. I do wish you luck. Now I just watch and give you the guidance I am supposed to. Also, guard you. Not that I need to."

The woman then disappears, and Duke is alone. The pit has a ladder that heads down towards another orange door. The lava that is reduced to a small puddle is moving towards the ladder. Duke must be quick. Sliding down the ladder, avoiding looking at the creepy thing beneath him, he makes it to the door with seconds to spare. It opens, and Duke jumps through it, slamming it shut behind him. Catching his breath before taking in the place before him.

Chapter Fourteen

A New Room

This place that Duke ran into is another room. There is a desk with a stool and supplies sitting on top of the table. Grabbing the water, he downs it. The thirst from the lava room is too much.

There is also food. Shocked at what he sees, Duke cannot eat. There in front of him is spaghetti bolognaise, set out just like his mum used to do it. A small salad on the side and a slice of pizza garlic bread tucked into it, cheese placed on top of the meat that is melting nicely. He is hungry but can't bring himself to touch it.

There is also a can of Diet Coke, which his mum used to love. Sitting there staring at it isn't doing any good, but he can't tear himself away.

Time passes slowly; the food remains untouched, yet it stays hot.

"I am not going to eat this."

There is no response. Not that he thought there would be.

"What am I supposed to do now?"

Realising that he just asks a question without hesitation, Duke is shocked at himself. The food vanishes, and in the place of it are an apple and a ham sandwich, with another bottle of water. The Diet Coke had disappeared, too. The question he asked has saved him from the torment.

"This place is so weird. I would think it a dream if not for the pain before. That lava fingers heat was unbearable." Duke talks aloud hoping the gorgeous guide is listening.

Which she is. Her heart is not being in the torture with this one. Duke seems so different from all the others. It is not fun to torture the already broken, especially when they still have so much light in them despite their past.

Showing herself, deciding a little push will not hurt.

"Duke? You should rest. There will be much ahead for you, and it is not going to be easy. This room is completed; there will be no more surprises here. I will provide more supplies for you and a mattress. Don't expect this compassion later. This is a one-off to get you started on the right foot."

Her sudden appearance startles Duke, but he was grateful for what she said and did.

"Thank you." That is all he could bring himself to say.

Before him, now there is a bag filled with water bottles and fruit. Some jerky and cheese and also a few bags of sweets. Sitting top is a note:

Use sparingly. Keep your wits about you, and good luck.

Duke folds up the note and keeps it in his jeans pocket. Looking around then, he sees a mattress on the floor with a pillow and blanket.

Deciding that he is way too tired to overthink, Duke makes his way to the makeshift bed, instantly falling asleep as soon as he gets under the blanket and lays down.

The guide watches Duke falls asleep. She is worried that a reprimand is coming her way but decided it is worth it. The others break rules all the time; this is her first.

The Next Part

Duke wakes up refreshed and confused. Remembering where he is then and jumps up. Looking at himself, his top is different. An orange t-shirt has replaced his own, and orange shorts are in the place of his jeans. The note is no longer there.

Picking up the bag of food, which is a makeshift cloth rucksack in the same orange colour, Duke walks around the room, looking for an exit while munching on a banana.

After looking everywhere, he decides to move the mattress. Under it is a trapdoor with no handle. There is a keyhole, and it is pretty big. So Duke continues to search. He looks around the desk, on it and under, but there is nothing, not even a draw to search.

Sitting on the chair, Duke tries to think. The chair is wobbly, and one of the legs does not sit right. A smile appears on Duke's face then.

Standing up, he pulls at the leg; it pops out. The leg is the handle, and the other end is the key.

Kneeling by the trapdoor, Duke slots the key into the hole; it fits perfectly. Twisting the leg and then pulling, the door opens revealing steps heading down towards a bright light.

"Well, that's interesting. I better get this over with. OK, beautiful guide, I am ready. I will see you at the next spot." With that last comment, Duke descends to his new destination.

Chapter Fifteen

Into the Light

Bright light surrounds Duke. He cannot make anything out. There is nothing but blinding white.

Closing his eyes, Duke tries to feel out his surroundings. Walking slowly with his arms outstretched, nothing comes within his reach. So he just keeps going. Now, with one hand covering his eyes, the light is starting to hurt, even with his eyes being closed.

Finally, his fingers encounters something, a hard surface that is really cold to touch. Slowly opening his eyes, Duke sees a blurred metal door. The light has dimmed enough for him to see without pain, but his eyes still have to focus. Taking a breath in, he pulls at a silver handle. The door opens smoothly, and darkness swallows him, yet Duke is not scared this time. The dark is actually a relief. If his eyes can sigh, they will have.

When Duke's eyes adjust to the change, he decides to feel his way around again. As he does, there is a dim light in the distance; it gradually comes closer and slowly lights up the room.

Another door is on the other side of a table; sitting by the door is a man, his head bowed and his hands resting on the floor. He looks to be resting. Or dead. Next to him is a box, orange like the other things. Duke is beginning to dislike that colour now.

As Duke heads over towards the man, he notices that there is crystal on the table. It looks to be Citrine. His mum loved collecting crystals before she started getting abused. Duke remembers that it is supposed to carry the power of the sun, a powerful cleanser that also provides warmth and energy, raises self-esteem and revitalises.

Duke then remembers all the times his mum would sit with him and talk about all the abilities of crystals. She would show him a book about it, and he got to feel all the different coloured ones. This orange was his favourite. His mum let him keep one, but the stepdad smashed it when Duke was alone with him and told his wife that her ungrateful son got angry and destroyed it. That was the last time, he was given a crystal. Duke could not tell his mum the truth, however much it pained him.

Coming out of his memories, Duke notices that the man is looking at him now although he has no eyes. There are holes where his eyes should be. The man has white hair and pale skin. The clothes he wears are made of silver and grey mesh. Like fine chainmail. There is a huge ring on his finger that looks to have a stone missing.

Duke then notices that the man has very long, sharp teeth. He has never seen anything like it before. Not like the fictional vampires you read about or watch in movies. This man has teeth like a shark. Or demon-like.

Duke has an idea; the stone on the table looks like it fit into the ring on the finger of that thing. There is nothing to stop him from getting it and placing it there. Duke's gut tells him that he should do it.

That is until the man starts to stand, sniffing the air and feeling around. Saliva is now dripping from his sharp teeth.

Duke knows that he is in trouble, and he is terrified. The thing in front of him must be about two feet taller than he was and twice as wide. There is no way to overpower him.

Duke then spots a knife sitting by the crystal. That is not there before. It is large and looks very sharp. Thinking about things, he knows that killing the thing is not something he wants to do. But, if he tries to fix the stone into its ring, Duke may lose some flesh.

"Don't kill me. I am going to help you. OK? This sucks."

Duke grabs the stone. He then gets to the man fast trying to grab the hand with a ring. The thing bites down on Duke's shoulder taking a chunk of flesh from him, blood pouring down Duke's back. As the man is distracted with the flesh, Duke places the stone in the ring. Bright red light engulfs the man-thing. When the light clears, there is a dark-haired man in the place of the once-scary beast. He is still tall, but he has amber eyes and normal teeth.

"Thank you. I lost the crystal that contains part of my soul. Without my sight, it was impossible to find it. Everyone became a threat, so the other form I carried took over. I apologise for trying to eat you. Without the stone I'm lost to my instincts. Nothing can bring me out of it. Most would have taken advantage of my blindness and killed me, taking the stone with them."

"I am not a killer." Duke knows he get rid of his stepfather's body and assists in the punishment. But he doesn't do the killing.

"No, you are not, are you? Well, young man, I must get back to my duties now that I am free to do so. The door is open and good luck." That is all the man said before vanishing.

"What is with none of you giving me your names?" Again, Duke does not realise he now asks questions without thinking.

Walking to the door, Duke grabs his bag of supplies. When he pulls it on his shoulder, he notices that the bite has healed. There is a massive scar, but no blood or gaping wound.

"This shit gets weirder and weirder."

After that statement, Duke opens the door that is all wood this time, no more silver or orange. Not yet anyway. Then he walks through.

This man is one to watch. All those watching are curious. Will he be different? Only time will tell, and there is plenty of that here. That and much more.

Chapter Sixteen

Getting Challenging

Hot, then cold. That is how Duke is feeling in this place. He is out in a field with burnt trees and charred grass. Sipping on his water and looking around, nothing really stands out. The air is cold, but near the trees and grass heat emanates. There is a path up ahead, no surprise it's orange.

"I guess that's the way I need to go."

"Yep," a voice answers him.

Duke looks for the source. There is the guide looking at him with no emotion on her stunning face.

"Hi, guide, long time no see," he jests.

"Hello, Duke. Well done so far. But that was easy compared to what is to come."

"Can you give me something else to call you? This no-name thing is killing me."

"I am sorry. In this place, names have power. Only Scarlett can give hers, as she welcomes our guests, and has no power here. You can call me G, short for guide or guard."

"OK, G it is. Better than nothing I guess."

"Right. I must give you the next bit of guidance. You must follow that path. Just keep going, do not veer off the path for anything unimportant. That is all I can give you for now."

She disappears again, leaving Duke to walk the path alone.

The journey starts off fine. There is nothing deterring him. There are still trees and grass, but some are aflame now. There are no animals though, which is a relief to Duke. The thought of them being hurt by the fire does not sit well. Innocents getting hurt makes Duke angry.

With that thought in mind, Duke sees something on the path ahead. There are these things that look to be on fire. With a closer inspection, he sees that they are made of fire. Balls with legs and little feet. More are in the field; they have caused the damage. Although cute, each one is deadly if touched. The few that block Duke's way are not willing to move.

Duke has nothing that he can use. Not willing to hurt the little critters. By the side of the field is a ditch, which has none of the creatures. Thinking about things that G told him, Duke weighs up his options. The path is blocked, to pass he would need to either get them to move or maybe use his water to stop them. Not willing to risk hurting them, Duke decides to try and find another way. Maybe running and jumping over them?

The small balls of fire start to bounce on their tiny feet. They look excited like it is a game to them.

Duke takes out water and pours it over his body, soaking himself. Then he runs as fast as he can towards them before taking a huge jump. The flames catch his shoes scorching them a little, but he is unharmed and so are they.

There is then a bright orange light that falls from above, landing right in front of Duke. The light transforms into a huge beast made up of fire and lava. The body is like that of a big cat; its head is shaped like a wolf with slightly rounder ears. Huge teeth that drip lava and a tail that is long with barbs that look deadly.

The beast steps towards Duke, who is not terrified. He is shaking with fear looking at this huge monster in front of him. Does he make a mistake? Should he have done something different?

Flames suddenly reduce from the beast's body, and the small balls of fire all gather around it. Their flames also get smaller. What is left is cute fluffy ginger, mini versions of the beast. It is also now just a glowing ginger fluffy thing, still huge but stunning and almost sweet.

Duke is stunned. The beast looks towards him and almost seems to be bowing.

G suddenly appears at the side of it, giving a hug to all of them.

"You really are something, Duke. These are my pets. Most would have tried to hurt them in some way. You chose the only option that wouldn't do harm, yet it could have hurt you. The mother is extremely grateful. She offers you safety through her realm. Herself or the babies will not harm you or let any other try while you are here. Just carry on down the path, until you come to your next destination."

Duke is stunned into silence and just nods. Looking down, he sees one of the babies has walked up to him. Without thinking, he reaches down and picks it up, stroking its little orange head. The little thing purrs like a cat and licks Duke's hand while snuggling into his chest.

"Well, look at that. You made a friend. These creatures do not usually take to humans." G tells him and then walks over taking the snoozing baby from Duke's arms.

"As cute as that is, you need to carry on with your journey. We shall meet at the next part."

Duke is suddenly alone again. Even the beast and her babies have disappeared. In the place of them are more supplies and a pair of boots. Duke then notices that his shoes have no soles. They must have melted when he jumped over the fireballs.

Once the new boots are on and food in his belly, Duke heads back down the path, wanting the next challenge to be soon, as it will be one step closer to getting out of the strange place.

The walk is going on for a long time. In the distance, trees are still aflame, and he can see many of the orange balls, but they stay away. It does feel a little cold now without them being close. Duke cannot help but wonder what the point is. All of this has no meaning to him. What is he being tested for?

Well, eventually, all will become clear.

Chapter Seventeen

Sleeping Enemies

Duke finally reaches the end of the road. He has no problems although there will have been a lot more challenges if it aren't for the promise from G's pet.

The new door is made of glass, yet there is no way to see through it. A knob is in the centre, which looks to be made of gold or something that resembles it. Duke reaches out to turn it, but he is instantly shocked. He looks for something else, but the door is just standing there in the middle of the path, with nothing holding it up and nothing behind it.

Touching the glass and feeling the coldness of it, Duke isn't sure what to do. He is really stumped this time.

Standing there looking for a solution, Duke feels something nudge his leg. The little critter that takes a liking to him is staring up at the man with big sad eyes.

"Hi, cutie. I don't think I can do this buddy. Do you want to share my jerky?" Sitting down by the door, they both enjoy the food. Duke avoids getting the water near his new friend, just in case.

With a full belly, he decides to try and open the door again, but his little friend gets there first and starts to flame up. The heat from it is stifling, making Duke step right back.

He sees then that the door is melting from the heat until there is nothing left but a puddle of melted glass and the golden knob. The ball of fire returns to its cute fluffy ball, gives Duke a lick on his leg, nudges the golden knob then runs off.

"Thank you, buddy," Duke calls out while picking up the knob. There is no shock this time. The little critter must have meant for him to take it with him. So, into his bag, it goes.

Stepping into the now open doorway, there is nothing but darkness. Yet that does deter him this time.

With each step, Duke feels that he is not alone. He can hear breathing and shuffling. Fear grips him now, as he has seen some of what this place holds in its depths.

There is not a light anywhere, so all that he can do is step carefully and try to avoid whatever is in the darkness. Old memories of being trapped in the dark surface. Pushing them down, Duke carries on, knowing that stopping now will be bad. He can feel it.

Light tapping can be heard in the distance. It is like liquid dripping onto a metal surface or water hitting the bottom of a sink. The thought of there being something in the distance other than the sleeping forms makes Duke worry a little less. That must be where he needs to go. Straining his ears, the sound becomes clearer. Heavy when they hit whatever the surface is. Dripping louder. It is not water, that's for sure.

There is a little light up ahead where the sound is coming from. It isn't much. But it allows Duke to see where the noise is coming from. It is a stainless-steel table, and on it lays a person; the drips are blood pooling into a bucket from a hole in his or her head. On closer inspection, Duke sees that it is a female, but her head has been shaved to allow for the hole, and she is covered in an orange sheet that is soaked in blood.

Fear hits when realisation dawns. The body is alive, and it looks like Julie. But that cannot be right, can it?

"Julie?" Duke asks as he attempts to touch the body on the cold metal table. Just as his hand is about to come in contact, someone grabs Duke's arm, spinning around.

Nothing can prepare him for what he sees in front of his eyes. The man who destroyed the lives of so many. The monster himself.

"Dad?"

"How dare you wake me, you selfish boy! This is my private space!"

The man swings his fist to hit Duke, but after years of being hit and then having to look after himself, the fist is dodged with ease. But that does not stop his stepdad. He carries on trying to land a hit.

As Duke avoids this, Julie starts to stand. Her arms outstretch reaching for the men. Her blood still runs down her pale face.

Duke turns to see her, and his heart stops for a second. Her eyes are no more there, just empty holes, just like the man he helped. Yet this time there is no crystal or door.

With each step towards Duke, Julie loses more blood. Yet she doesn't slow down. His stepdad has stopped trying to land a hit and headed in Julie's direction.

"No, old man, not this time," Duke says as he stands in front of Julie. Then strikes before the woman can be hurt.

"She is mine to hurt now boy, you left her alone to suffer. Even in death, her body shall benefit me. Her organs will fetch a good price."

Duke no longer sees Julie but his mother. The anger takes over then, and he strikes the man before him. With each strike, the body of his mother starts to heal, until his stepdad is a bloody mess on the floor.

Feeling a gentle hand on his shoulder, Duke turns around. There is his mother, whole, and smiling at him.

"I love you," she says before vanishing.

"Mum!" Duke cries, but she has gone. So has the man he used to call Dad. Nothing remains now, just a metal table and a bucket that no longer holds any blood. The silence is deafening.

G watches on with tears in her eyes.

"What the hell! We do not cry," she reprimands herself.

Meanwhile, Duke gets himself together and tries to find a way out. The darkness starts to lift completely, letting him see the place around him. There is not much to see. It looks like a morgue. White walls and steel tables. Draws in the wall that must hold bodies.

Scalpels litter the empty tables along with scissors and gauze that is red with blood.

"I need to get out of here."

As he continues to search, it dawns on him that the place is small, yet he has been walking for ages, and that monster is asleep somewhere, so there must be another room that he cannot see. Feeling along the walls and trying to remember the way he came, Duke finds something or a wall that is not there. His hand passes straight through it. But going that way that would lead him back, not forward. So he turns around, and the draws look strange. Walking over to them and feeling each one, Duke finds that half of them are also an illusion. This is the way forward. Taking a large step through, Duke begins to fall.

Well, now, let us hope he survives the drop.

Chapter Eighteen

After the Fall

Duke is contemplating his decisions as he heads deeper into the darkness. There is no light at all making the fall seem longer. Should he have looked for another exit? Before he can panic even more there is a light. It is reflecting off a pool of silver liquid, which is what Duke is falling towards. Gravity does not seem to have any rules here. The descent is way too slow for the amount of time he was falling. Not something that crossed his mind, however.

The silver pool is beautiful. Duke cannot take in the beauty, the only thing on his mind is surviving the drop. He cannot swim, and the liquid looks thick.

When he finally hits the surface Duke bounces off it. The Consistency of the liquid is that of rubber, not liquid at all. When he has stopped bouncing, Duke lets out a sigh, then looks around as he catches his breath. Everything is silver. There is a single lamp that lights up the room, reflecting off the metallic surfaces. The only other colour is the orange draw that resides on a huge desk.

After crawling over to the edge of the pool, Duke climbs onto the solid surface, which is not easy. It is like a giant stress toy.

Finally, he gets to the draw and tries to open it. No surprise, it does not open. There is a small hole at the front of it.

Remembering the golden knob, Duke decides to try it. Pulling it out of his bag with care he tries to fit it into the small hole. The draw instantly grips onto the golden orb, and sparks emit from it.

The whole room lights up then. Everything turns white for a second, then dims to an orange glow. On the desk sits a small bag, the draw no longer there.

Opening the bag Duke sees some more jerky and water. A note is also in there.

This is for your journey, use it sparingly. This room is safe for you to rest for a while. You have deactivated all the traps with that orb. If you hadn't, the note would not have appeared to you.

Take your time, you will need your strength.

Take the stairs when you're ready. The journey ahead will not be as easy.

You have made friends and got help, however, what is coming needs to be completed by you alone.

Good luck Duke.
I'll be watching.
G

This doesn't help Duke's nerves. He is terrified now. If all that he went through was easy, the next tasks must be bad.

Sitting by the desk and drinking a little water, Duke is tempted just to stay there, but he knows that the food and water will eventually run out and he will have nothing left for the journey.

"Thank you, G. But I would rather go home."

Knowing that she will not reply, Duke decides to have a kip. So, after lying down on the floor, which is exactly what he does, using the bag as a pillow.

Hours pass, and the room gets dark. The only light is a small orange glow coming from the pool. There is now a hole where the bouncy liquid once resided. In the hole is a set of steps descending into the light.

Once Duke rises, he notices this. After the last walk into a light, the lad is hesitant.

"Come on, man, you can do this. You have been through worse."

The pep talk seems to work. Duke heads towards the steps slowly. Each step has made him shake more with fear. Yet it does not stop him. Down he goes until there are no more steps, just an archway where the light is coming from. Walking through it, Duke feels a pull. He is then dragged into an orange light.

A freezing wind wraps around him, numbing his fingers and face. Tears pour from his eyes only to form icicles. The breath leaving his lungs feels cold, as well as the saliva in his mouth.

Everything hurts now, his organs failing him the blood in his veins now freezing. No words can leave his frozen mouth.

Darkness overtakes him then. Memories of being freezing in that she'd come to mind as he drifts into oblivion.

Chapter Nineteen

Is This the End?

Warmth spreads through Duke now. The pain that comes with the freezing winds has gone. The light is still there, glowing orange and taunting him.

"Am I dead? G, answer me. You want questions? Well, there it is!"

"Hi, Duke. This isn't your end, yet. You had to be frozen to pass through the fire unharmed. There was nothing I could do. I am sorry for your pain. We do not apologise usually, so take it. This appearance wasn't supposed to happen either. I will be in trouble for responding to you. Just know that this is all happening for a reason. That is all I can say. Now go and finish this you annoying human."

"Human? What do you mean? That is the second time you have referenced humans. Are you not one? Hello? Oh, she's gone again, and I'm back talking to myself. Nice work, Idiot."

Duke takes in his new surroundings again. Each room has that grey, silver and orange look. Yet this one is red and very warm. Hot aches are running through the now warm body, and all the blue has now turned bright red.

All around are red stones that look like glowing rubies. The walls are solid rock with tiny glittering specks of the same stone. The doorway he must have arrived through has a fire blocking it, the flames are white. The heat from it is stifling, even from the distance he is at.

There are no windows. Each wall is solid-looking with no holes. The stones do not move, and they are warm to touch.

Nothing stands out that can give a clue as to what he needs to do. A memory then appears in his mind. The shed. When it is hot out, the metal prison will heat up and burn Duke's delicate skin. Its door is so hot that the handle will burn when touched. Duke often wishes that he has some water to pour on the hot surface to give him a reprieve.

An idea comes to Duke then. Opening his bag and taking out a bottle, he walks over to the fire.

Realising that this was his way in, Duke turns and looks around for anything that could be an illusion. Feeling the walls, nothing happens. His hands just hit a rock.

Opening the bottle then, he pours some of the liquid on the wall. Steam fills the room, and the red stones shake a little. Then they stop moving, and the room heats up more.

"Oh, come on."

This time, the liquid gets poured onto the stones. Each one that gets water explodes, the shards digging into the stone wall and into Duke's flesh.

There amongst the debris is a small button. Looking closer, Duke sees that there is one at either side of the room. One blue and one red. The wall starts to crack. Two doors appear, the same colour as the buttons.

With blood pouring down the cuts, he has a job to see as some get into his eyes. The doors look identical apart from the colour.

Red or blue? He looks at them and thinks hard. Duke hates blue, his stepdad's car was blue. The one that was used to take him away from the safety of school and into the hell of being at home.

Red is the colour of all the blood he has seen, both from his own body and the mum he loved so much. Blue was the lesser of two evils, so that is what he took.

Pressing the button, there is a loud bang, and the blue door swings open, revealing what looks to be a swimming pool, the same one at his old school.

Without thought Duke walks into the building. The cool water looks refreshing. Not being able to swim made things difficult, especially when his friends loved to play and dive.

The door vanishes leaving Duke to explore the place that also haunted him. Somewhere that makes him not want to learn swimming or anything that his teacher wanted him to do.

Each day, there is worse than the shed. At least at that place, he is alone.

One of the girls he likes has her dad with her. He will volunteer to take Duke under his wing. While the teacher teaches the others that can swim, Duke will go and learn in the toddler's pool. His crush's dad is supposed to help. But that is not the case.

Each lesson gets worse. The man likes to taunt Duke. Not the way his dad did. No, this man is bad in a different way. He does not like young girls, so his daughter is safe. However,

Duke is the ideal victim. Unloved and often beaten, he becomes a target.

Things get bad. Touches and caresses. Duke is told that he is special; that is why all the attention is on him alone, and the others are jealous that they do not get 'quality time'.

This goes on for months; nothing has gone further than touches. The girl keeps asking Duke to come over and sleep at her house. Knowing that nothing bad can happen at school, Duke has declined and just spent time with the monster when he has those so-called lessons.

His teacher often asks if Duke is ready to join the others in the big pool. Excuses are always given.

"He won't listen."

"He is not willing."

"Duke is too scared to swim in the big pool."

The horrid man always finds an excuse. That is until Duke tells his dad that he loves swimming so much. The lessons are then stopped, the hatred from his stepdad helping him this time.

A year later, however, Duke finds out that a young boy is found raped and killed, along with the girl. She walks in on her father hurting the boy when she hears strange noises coming from the spare room. The evil ass is made out to be a victim with his daughter being killed, too.

Duke doesn't come forward. He is too ashamed. His young mind does not comprehend the devastation of his silence. There are many victims after, ones that can have been prevented. The man's wife is not around. She works as an air hostess and never comes home. Especially when her daughter was killed. Being away seems to make it less real for her.

Duke has not thought about all that in a while. The monster is never caught. There are just bodies that are found. All males.

Guilt hitting Duke hard then. That part of his life is blocked out. He has forced himself to forget. Now, he needs to face that decision he made, one that could have prevented so many ruined lives.

Chapter Twenty

Repercussions of a Bad Decision

This is it, the time that all the past misdeeds come forth. You cannot bury your past forever. One way or another it will come back to haunt you. Sometimes when we least expect it. A really good person like Duke has skeletons just like the rest of them. Turning a blind eye to evil is never a good thing.

"OK. What do I do here?"

Again, no reply. There is nothing to do but look around. The main area is clear. Nothing different. The toddler pool is set in another part with a wall separating it from the large pool looks very different. There is blood instead of water, and dark lumps are floating in the bright red liquid.

On closer inspection, Duke sees that the lumps are moving. They are heads, with sharp teeth like a shark. They even have a tail, but the heads are human. Boys to be exact. Sitting on the poolside there is a man covered in blood, he has the same teeth, although the rest of him is human. His skin is also red, so you cannot make out the blood from the flesh. It is the monster, the smug, evil villain that haunts kids' dreams.

"You?"

He turns his head after hearing Duke. A creepy smile spreads across his face. Blood pours from his mouth as he does.

The heads jump up from the pool now, trying to get a look at the newcomer.

"These are all your victims. What the hell have I done? Why was I such a coward? Let them go! Release them you evil asshole."

Behind the man, a beautiful woman appears. She has long dark red hair, the bluest eyes and pale, flawless skin. An adult version of the girl he knew.

"Make it right," she says before throwing an item to Duke.

Catching it, he sees that it is a knife made of the same orange crystal that he loved. When he turns to thank her, the beast has her in his grasp. He suddenly tares off her head and tosses it into the pool and then proceeds to feed her body to the others.

"Noooooo! You asshole. You will pay for that!"

Laughing the monster lowers himself into the pool.

"I do not kill, but this time it is needed. All those innocent lives. Yes, I should have said something. But I was a scared kid too. That was what you counted on. The hate from my father overshadowed the need to help others. Letting you get away with those horrid crimes."

Duke then dives into the pool, the heads all moving towards him, taking bites from his body. But that didn't stop him. Duke lunges for the beast of a man. Then plunges the knife into the heart of the evil being before the heads finish tearing him apart. The beast now writhing in agony, and slowly dissolving into the water.

"Death is painful." Duke thinks to himself.

But he doesn't get out of this that easy.

Opening his eyes, and looking up, there are loads of faces staring down at him.

"What the hell happened? How am I still here?"

"You cannot die in this place, but you can feel the pain of it."

"G? What, how?"

"Easy, your body has been through a lot. You are put back together, but it will take a while to fully function."

Duke notices then that there are children all around him. Boys of different ages.

"Thank you," they all say smiling, then disappearing before his eyes.

One remains. The beautiful woman, Duke's first crush.

"Forgive yourself, Duke. You freed us. I am forever grateful. My first crush is a hero now. live for us all." Her last words before she vanishes.

"All those kids, G. Why?"

"That isn't something I can answer I'm afraid. Just know that what you did was brave, you knew that in going after him, you wouldn't get out, but did it anyway. I must go, but your next task awaits. Keep going Duke, your end is closer than you think."

"OK. Goodbye, G."

Duke sits up and notices that he is back in the hot room. One door, the red one awaits him.

"Right, here I go again."

Pressing the red button and then walking through the scary doorway.

Hold on for this one, Duke may be getting to the end, but it isn't the last of his story. His path is far from finished.

Chapter Twenty-One

Scary Red Door

Stepping into the next place is hard. Duke is right to worry about this one.

Dark red walls dripping with goo surround him. Echoes of the past invade his mind. Whispers of harsh words are spoken to him and the screams from his mother's pain. Visions appear in front of him, apparitions of all the abuse his mum faced. The men that violated her, right in front of him, but Duke is unable to do anything.

"Stop this, please. I cannot see this."

His pleas go unanswered. G is watching with sad eyes. She is forbidden to interfere in this.

Duke's heart is breaking seeing his mother's last moments, terrified and in so much pain. Covering his head with his hands, Duke drops to the floor in tears.

"Please stop."

The images then change. They show his stepdad running into the room shouting at the man who strangled her.

"What have you done? I let you have her for a minute of pleasure, not to take her life." Duke's stepdad screams at the man and punches him, knocking the murderer to the floor. He then sits on the bed and pulls the body of his wife towards himself.

"Wake up, baby, I am so sorry. This wasn't supposed to happen. I was desperate. Please wake up. What have I done? I love you, baby. I really do. Please I'll change; just wake up. I beg you."

Duke is shocked at the words he has heard. It doesn't matter. That man is a monster in every way.

All he can see in the apparition now is that man's tear-stained face.

"Take it back, please. All of it. Let me start again. Me, my wife and Duke. This addiction has taken what could have been an amazing life. Please someone help me. I realise now what I've become. I will do anything." The man begs.

Emotions flood through Duke. He didn't know of any addictions. Not that it changes what happened. His mother is still dead, and Duke's childhood is ruined.

"Is he forgiven, Duke? Does he deserve a second chance?" G's voice echoes in the room, but she doesn't appear.

"His childhood was worse than yours, creating a vicious circle. He wasn't as strong as you. That man took different substances to escape his reality, and the past that haunted him."

"It isn't for me to forgive him G. That is for my mother. Maybe my abuse can be forgiven but doing that to my mother. How can I forgive that? And nothing will be forgotten. If he had his life over without the abuse and ended up a different person. I don't know. All I can think of now is my mum's screams and her beautiful face full of terror. How can I think of forgiveness with that image playing through my mind on repeat."

That man's face is still floating around the room, tormenting Duke. The image splits, and the new face transforms into a different emotion until the room is full of them. Duke is sitting on the floor now, rocking with his head between his knees.

"Make it stop now, G. I will forgive the treatment of me, but never the pain he caused my mother. Nothing will change my mind about that."

Everything then turns orange, and all the faces disappear. The warm light is soothing and calming. The room is now filled with those orange crystals, all gleaming bright.

"Well done, Duke, you completed the journey in record time and without cheating."

"Can I go home now?"

"I am sorry, but your path doesn't end yet, just this journey."

"What does that mean, G?"

"You will see. Just rest now and all will be revealed at the end."

Duke is then transported to the room he started in. The clothes he had on originally are back on his body.

"Welcome back, Duke. I hear your journey was eventful. Sleep while your companions finish. There will be food bought up to you and something to drink." That male voice from the start booms into the room.

Laying on the bed, very exhausted Duke rests. Not knowing that something big will be coming his way.

Chapter Twenty-Two
Room One, Amy's Journey

Back at the reception area, the remaining two are waiting for their rooms. Benny suggests that Amy pick next, wanting to get in her good graces.

"Amy, you go. I don't mind waiting a little longer. You can treat me to a coffee later as thanks," Benny says while grinning.

"OK, if you are sure."

Amy then steps forward; there sits the remaining keys. One of them instantly draws her eye. It is an old rusty teal key, the same colour as her first car that was bought by her late grandmother. All many good memories from then, so that is the one that she decides on.

"Your choice is made. Follow your guide to the room Amy and have fun," Scarlett tells her while pointing to an extremely handsome man, now holding the bags. He looks like the others with almost black hair and cobalt eyes. But this man looks kinder somehow, and he smiles, the others do not.

Amy follows down a corridor. He keeps looking back to make sure that Amy is right behind him.

"Amy, you are in room number one. It is right at the front." His eyes have a little hesitancy in them.

"OK, thank you," she replies.

They come to a lift, it is the same colour teal as the key, but newer. There is no rust, which Amy is thankful for. That wouldn't make a good impression.

"Why do we need a lift? If it is number one, shouldn't it be on the ground floor?" Amy asks.

"No, you may have figured it out by now, but this isn't your average place."

"Oh, OK, sure."

Entering the lift, Amy does not see any buttons or numbers. There is only a shiny surface. The man places his hand against the side, and the lift starts to move. Not up or down, but to the side. Amy loses her footing, not expecting it to go that way. Her Guide catches her, making a blush form.

"I'm so sorry." That is all she can say. Her guide not moving for a little while.

"That is OK. It was my fault. I should have told you to hold on." Is he blushing too?

"What do I call you?"

"We cannot give you our names Amy. I am sorry. But you can call me De? I am your guide, so it is some of the letters. Or something similar?"

"No names? That is weird. I guess De it is then."

This journey is going to be complicated. It seems De, as he wants to be called, is smitten with the lovely Amy.

The lift stops, and the door opens into a room. De walks in and puts the bags on a bed.

The whole room is beautiful. The walls are cream, with teal pictures and silver mirrored draws. The bed is silver, with a chrome finish. The bedding is teal satin with a silver-coloured bottom sheet. There is a single wardrobe and a desk which are also mirrored. The carpet is a soft, thick cream that your feet sink into.

"I chose well. This place is beautiful."

"I am glad that you like it, Amy. Please take care and just be yourself. I am so sorry for what you will go through, and that you won't hate me. I have a feeling our paths are entwined." Before Amy could respond, De had vanished. Leaving her alone in the room.

Deciding that she feels a little tired, Amy lays on the bed to take everything in. Wanting to think about what De told her. What does it all mean?

But she did not get a chance. Everything went dark.

"Hello? Great, a power cut on our first day. Oh, well, sleep it is then."

"I am sorry, Amy, but sleep isn't an option yet." The voice from the other rooms echoes and makes Amy jump.

"What? Who?"

"You will find out eventually. Just sit back and enjoy the show. More will become clear. Amy, you have some tasks to follow. Should everything go well, your path will end, and you can go home."

"What does that mean?"

There was no answer, just flashes of light. One side of the wall lights up, and a recording starts to play.

Chapter Twenty-Three

Hidden Fears

The recording plays, and Amy sees herself playing in a garden that she recognises as her grans. There are three little black Scottie dogs running around with her. Amy is around two, and very active. Her love of all living things shows at an early age. Her heart is so large that everyone she meets loves her, including animals.

Amy's gran watches the girl play and smiles at the sight. Her pride shows through her elderly eyes, seeing how much like her daughter this little girl is. Everything from her blue eyes to the light emanates from her soul.

The picture then changes to Amy's mother. A beautiful lady is shopping with a man. They are looking at cakes. The man is Amy's stepfather. He is handsome with golden hair and green eyes that sparkle. So much love between them.

Amy cannot remember when her stepdad came into their lives. She only knows that her life is complete with him in it. He loves her like his own and dotes on Amy and her mother.

The image flicks to the pair carrying the cake that was chosen, with a huge candle on it showing the number Eighty-three. Amy is in a highchair clapping as her parents sing Happy Birthday to the older female. A very happy moment.

De watches this also, he is smiling at the happy sight.

"Why do we need to do this with her? Can we not forget this one?"

"She is here for a reason. Let us watch." All eyes are then back on the images playing.

Amy has tears in her eyes.

There is a change in the images, it is when Amy is given the car; she is fifteen.

"Your dad will need to fix this up, but it will be ready for when you need to take lessons Amy sweetheart."

"Thank you, Nanny. It is perfect. I love it, and I love you so much for getting it for me. You didn't have to. Dad, is that OK? What kind of car is it?"

"It is a Ford Capri, sweetheart. And a beauty."

"I cannot wait to start driving it, Dad. Isn't Nanny awesome?"

"That she is."

The next part plays, and the sight of it has Amy sobbing. They are in a hospital room, wires coming from her gran, who is pale and sweating.

She looks so frail while her family hold her hands.

Amy is nineteen here, and training to be a nurse at college to please her Nan. Although she wanted to be a Vet.

"Can I talk to my granddaughter alone?" she asks her children-in-law.

"Of course." Both say as they leave Amy.

Her Gran looks at the crying woman with such love.

"Amy, I am beyond proud of you. Whatever you say will not change that. OK? But I need to ask something of you. I am in so much pain, I've tried to hold on, but it is too much. I'm not asking you to help me die. I just wonder if you can accidentally leave me too many pills. Or put something on my table that I can take? Help me to go in peace. Please?"

"Nanny, you cannot ask me that, I will lose everything I have worked towards. You know that I love you, but that is something I cannot do. Even if it is you taking your life, I would be complicit in this. I can ask if the doctor can give you extra pain relief. I am sorry, I just couldn't live with myself."

"That is OK, dear. I understand. It was a lot to ask I know."

Amy watches the screen while sobbing her heart out.

"I should have helped her. She suffered so much after that," Amy tells herself, not knowing that she can be heard.

Looking back at the screen she sees that her mother is in the room now talking to her gran. Amy does not like the look on her mother's face. There is no sound coming from the film now. But it looks like they are having a heated conversation. Shortly after that the women embrace and Amy sees her mother's tears, nodding at whatever the older lady is asking.

"No, Mum, you didn't?"

Amy realises what she is seeing then. Because she refuses to help, her gran asks the same question of her mother. It must have been a week later, as her gran is very thin. She also refuses to see anyone for a while after Amy refuses to help. Until that day when they all say their goodbyes. Her mother is different after her death. The light she carries faded and the jokes she always makes stopped. Everyone thinks that it is grief, but now Amy knows the truth. Guilt then takes over. Her mother cannot forgive herself.

Now knowing what she did, her mother leaving with her husband makes sense. They have moved to Europe shortly after Amy has started university the following year. Wanting a new start.

Does she break her mother by refusing to help? Is her love not strong enough?

The recordings stop then, and the lights come back on.

"Amy, you only have a short look into your past, as there aren't many things that need to be addressed. You will start your journey now. We will meet again. Good luck."

There is something different about this woman. Her biological father is a mystery to all.

"Amy, are you OK? I will show you where to begin," De asks as he appears in the room again.

"What is this place, De? Why am I here?"

"I cannot answer that, Amy. I am so sorry. You will know eventually I swear."

"Why do I feel comfortable with you, De? Shouldn't I fear you or at least be wary of you?"

"You should, I suppose, but I don't want you to."

Doing something forbidden, De hugs Amy. Then instantly pulls away when he realises.

"Come this way, Amy. A door waits for you." De directs her to a small teal door which is situated on the wall by the lift. Opening it to reveal a long white corridor.

"Go ahead, Amy. Here is a bag of supplies that will help along the way. Again, please forgive me for what you must go through. I will help when I can."

Amy takes the bag and walks through the door, not looking at De as she does. Still shocked from the hug and the feelings that ran through her while she was in his arms.

Chapter Twenty-Four

A Confusing Place This Is

Amy walks down the white corridor. As she looks back, the teal door has vanished, along with De. There is nothing but white walls and a smooth white path. The light that illuminates the passage is coming from the walls, not a fixture.

Amy decides to delve into the bag. Looking down, she notices that her clothes are different. Instead of the dress she was in, there is now a teal and white outfit. A flowing white skirt and a teal bodice over a puff sleeves top. On her feet are teal ballet flats. Her long dark hair is up in a high ponytail.

"How?" she asks nobody in particular.

The bag has a lot in it. There are cookies, bottles of water, fruit, crisps, sweets and what looks to be jerky. Nothing that can help her here. When Amy raises her head, the walls have changed. Now they are yellow, with teal patterns on each of them. Rubbing her eyes, to see if she is imagining it. But they are the same. Each brick has a symbol.

"Great, I'm rubbish at puzzles."

The symbols look like insects. It does not bother her. She has no fear of anything, be it animal, insect or reptile. The walls then move. No, not the walls, the pictures are coming to life.

Amy puts her hands out, letting the creepy Crawleys climb over them. She smiles and starts to talk to the creatures, that to anyone else would be scary with their huge pincers and dripping venom.

"You are beautiful. I've never seen anything like you before."

The onlookers are shocked.

"Why are they not attacking? Guide, have you something to do with this? She should be writhing in agony, not playing with the things. They should cause the same pain as her gran had at the end."

"It is not my doing, they seem to like her. Each not wanting to cause her pain," De tells the onlooker, trying not to smile.

"If they will not harm her, what use are they? Take her to the next place. Make sure she feels all that pain. Use one of the dead ones, they have no feelings."

"They are not on her journey. She doesn't deserve to be devoured by them."

"Do it."

De is reluctant, but he does as he is asked.

Amy is suddenly caught in darkness. The creatures go back to their lifeless forms on the bricks.

When the light comes back on, Amy is no longer in the corridor, but a room. There are several doors scattered around. Some even on the ceiling, and trapdoors on the floor. a few windows look out onto a deserted street, with strange things moving around from building to building. They look like zombies, yet they seem to be intelligent. Knowing how to open doors and climb into cars. It is a scary sight. Each one looks to be a different colour. The skin on some is blue, others yellow, and the large ones that look the slowest are red, and some skinny ones are purple which run around with great speed.

Something tells Amy not to leave this room. Her gut screaming at her that it is not safe out there. Deciding to agree with it, she decides to try each door and see what is in them.

The first one Amy decides to try is the trapdoor, as it is closest to her. Before she takes the handle, there is a firm hand on her shoulder pulling her away from it.

"Don't, not that one." It is De.

"What is happening, De? This should freak me out, but it all feels familiar. Who are you? What are you?"

De is silent; he just looks at Amy, trying to figure her out.

"I don't know. Really, I don't. Just try to trust me; I am going to do whatever I can. This is going to be bad. There are keys to these doors. Don't go for the obvious ones. The keys are out there though inside the dead ones. That is what we call them; they have no souls or feelings. Each just exists without a real purpose."

"That is so sad. The poor things."

"Do not pity them. They destroy whoever is different, without thought. And with brutality."

De holds Amy's hand then and places a knife in it. He vanishes straight after leaving Amy more confused than ever.

The knife is yellow in colour with a silver line going down the middle of it. The handle is also yellow.

"I had better go out there then. How do I do that?" The large window then opens.

"That way I guess." Amy then begins to climb out of it and is hit with the smell of decay.

Chapter Twenty-Five

Fear Like No Other

Amy takes in her surroundings. The place is bleak and empty apart from the creatures in the distance.

This task is not designed for her. This woman is not a fighter. De is terrified for her. These things obey nobody, and they love the taste of innocence. Each colour has a unique gift of torment. All of them hold a key; none will let them go.

Holding the knife in her hands, Amy makes her way over to the rundown buildings, her hands shaking as she does.

"Yellow, I need to get a yellow person," she quietly tells herself.

The creatures then start to notice her. Each one turns towards the direction Amy stands.

A fight then starts between them all. It is brutal. They are tearing each other apart. Blue creatures are holding back, they look to be waiting, hiding behind items and doors. Purple beings run towards her, but the yellow tear them apart easily. They are vicious, with teeth that are red with the blood of the victims dripping down onto their yellow chests. None have clothes on, just torn rags hanging down their disgusting bodies. At one point, the rags must have been clothing.

The red dead ones are the first to be torn up. They are big but slow. Body parts now litter the empty streets. Blue and yellow are the only ones remaining. With blue still hiding, the yellow home in on their target. Amy.

"Amy, hide, please," De's voice is now whispering in her ear, but she cannot see him. "Run sweet girl. They are not the smartest, so outsmart them. Worry about the blue, they are smart."

"De?" she asks before deciding to take his advice, running as fast as she can to another building.

She finds an abandoned cinema. Seats have been torn out, and the screens destroyed. Thankfully, the door closes.

Getting her breath back, Amy tries to produce a plan. Knowing that she will never raise her hand to hurt any living thing.

Looking at the knife she knows that it may be the case. How can she hurt them?

Deciding to find another way, Amy walks around the place. Stair's head to another level, so she walks up them, hoping to find something.

Several doors are off the hinges. One is still intact with a key in the lock.

Amy turns the knob, which does not open. Turning the key then, which lets her in. Slowly, she takes out the key and takes it in the room with her. A dim light from a small window illuminates the space. There isn't much, just a desk, a chair, a set of drawers and some dead flowers in a broken vase.

Looking through the desk, Amy finds some books. They are all handwritten, with pictures of each dead one. After locking the door, she starts to read.

Just as Amy starts, there is a weird sound coming from outside. Peaking out the window, the sight is horrid.

The dead ones are searching for her. The bodies that were torn apart are reforming, leaving behind blood trails. She can see the blue looking up at the buildings, they scare her the most. The others can be outsmarted.

Taking a deep breath, Amy sits back down and starts to read the books:

The Dead Ones

What I have found thus far is that each colour has a meaning. There isn't much time left for me, so I hope this information helps someone.

There are four colours that I can see so far.

Blue; these seem to be highly intelligent; they know I am here, yet they wait. Each seems to communicate with each other by hand signals, simple yet effective.

There have been many people coming through this place. Each is torn apart and eaten, only to reform as one of them, or reformed as themselves, and having to start this path again.

I can see the agony in the eyes of the victims.

Watching each of them perform helps in my task. Work out a way to escape and find a key.

To get a key I need to find the knife that will kill one of them permanently.

Then find the room that I appeared in first.

This place changes to suit the person, so I can never find a place to leave yet.

Stealing from someone didn't work either. The key vanished as soon as my hand touched it.

Amy puts the book down then. This doesn't look good. She must kill one of them or stay here and rot. There isn't a body, so maybe he or she got free.

Taking another notebook, Amy starts to read again hoping that there is something in it.

After several failed attempts at following someone, I have realised that only they can go out of the door they opened. There is a way out, I just must do the work myself.

People coming in have been less frequent, so food is scarce now.

Following my previous notes, the colours.

Yellow; whoever must kill these will have difficulty. They are lethal and vicious.

Nothing stops them. You can cut off a head, and the head will instantly reconnect.

I have seen many men who have been torn apart in seconds by these, without a chance to stab them.

The yellow knives are rare, never in my time here have I seen one. The men I have spoken to also have never seen one on the hunt. Yellow is the most sought-after though, as it takes you to a door that holds good things. So each member wants to find one. Or should I say, victim?

Next is Red; slow and stupid is all I can say of these. Although strong, they are easily taken down. When reforming these dead ones is even slower, it takes a whole day.

The red key will not take you anywhere good, as it is an easy task, so the next door will be just as challenging.

Purple: Well, you cannot catch these easily. Fast and nimble, but not that smart. They are easy to kill if you can get one.

One of the men I spoke with said there is supposed to be a white key, it is hidden in a yellow. The worst of them, large fast and even more deadly than the others, travels alone, instead of staying with those of their colour.

I have not come across this, but I am looking out for that yellow knife just in case.

One thing that I have noticed is that no women enter here. Having female company would be nice, as this is the only place in which others are seen. That is unless they work for those who put us here.

"No women? De, what am I doing here then?" Amy asks, but she gets no reply.

De is beside himself. He wants to get her out of there; she doesn't belong in such a place. Yet he is forced to wait and watch, knowing what Amy will have to endure.

Chapter Twenty-Six

Nowhere to Hide

Amy looks over the other notebooks; they are all gibberish now, not making any sense to her. They are just ramblings and nothing helpful.

Looking through the other draws, nothing stands out. Just a few pens and some empty notebooks. There is also another key with a label on it.

Food store

"He must have left this here."

Amy then takes a pad and some pens to make notes of this place, while she searches.

There is plenty of food left in her bag for now, so Amy replenishes herself before heading to find this place. Maybe there will be something other than food, some information perhaps.

After looking out into the corridor to see if it is clear, Amy decides that now is the time to leave. She runs down the hallway, looking for another locked door. There are broken projectors and what looks like dry blood all over the floors.

She can see some red, dead ones wandering downstairs. They do not look up; with no idea she is there.

On one side of the wall, there is a hint of yellow. Seeing this Amy knows that she needs to move and find this room.

Running down the corridor now with haste. Each door is open already or broken. The hallway is long, and it gets thinner the further she goes. There are no more stairs anywhere and it is getting darker. If they find her here, there is nowhere she can hide.

When Amy thinks that all hope is lost and she will be found, there is a small light up ahead. It is cobalt blue, like De's eyes. Trusting her gut again, she follows the light. It leads her to a small door that she wouldn't have been able to find, it was hidden behind a tall plastic plant, with no light near it. The blue lamp or orb that was there vanished as soon as the door was spotted.

Feeling her way now, Amy found the keyhole. Opening the door then to find that it is a lounge. A brown leather sofa sits by one wall, it looks comfy. A small table sits by it with some water bottles and crisps on it. There is also a kettle and a jar of coffee on a separate table. A blanket is folded on the sofa with a pillow on top.

A small fridge sits on another surface and a cupboard above that. Looking inside Amy sees that it is full of food, also some dry milk powder. There are some biscuits and chocolate, along with tins of fruit and soup. There is also veg and beans, jerky and sugar. Plenty to last her if she stays a while.

But she won't. Her friends would be waiting on her return.

There are several draws to search, but Amy gets really tired. After locking the door, she falls asleep on the comfortable sofa.

Screaming then wakes her. It is loud and terrifying. Making her way over to the window that she didn't realise was there, Amy sees the dead ones fighting over something. It is a man, and he is terrified. There is a purple fighting with a red, and several more reds are coming. The man needs to get out of there. Amy wants to help, but the window is nailed shut, and the glass is unbreakable.

Unable to do anything but watch the horror. The poor man is being torn and eaten by the reds. The purple one has been thrown away in pieces that are starting to reform. The screaming is coming from the reds, they are calling the others for food. The man has stopped moving now. There is nothing left of him.

Amy cannot look away, tears streaming down her face.

Slowly the beasts move away, and a body starts to appear. The victim is returning, his body coming back and taking shape. There are yellows coming towards him. Just as he is back into a human form, they start to descend. And the carnage starts again.

Screaming to herself and dropping to the floor. That book was right; those yellow are savage; they didn't even give him a chance.

Taking out the yellow knife, Amy knows that she must take one out, get it alone and find the key.

The only way to do that is to draw one to her. Then she must find her way back to the room of doors. A plan forms in her mind.

Taking out a pad, she begins to figure out how to do this, she also makes a map of the outside that she can see. Marking off each building. It hasn't changed for her, even though the note made it seem that it did.

The man is no longer there. Blood splatter is all that is left. A few blues are looking around, maybe hunting for him.

Amy takes in the features of the blues then. It is hard to see much from where she is, but she can see that they look human. The bodies of the blues are lean, and they are tall. Their faces look alike, the only difference being some are taller than others. The top of their heads is large, without hair, just smooth skin covering the big brains.

Looking around again, Amy finds some binoculars and a torch. Knowing that they will come in handy, she places them in her bag. There are also some rope, tape and a small penknife.

Amy decides to try the kettle. Weirdly it works. There is a large battery attached to it. No electricity, however. The fridge has more water, and another battery pack makes it work.

A few cups sit in the food cupboard, so Amy makes a drink and savours the taste while she can. It isn't great, but it is coffee.

Putting everything into her bag that she could carry, Amy heads out, ready to face it all. A plan is all set.

She will lure a yellow to the small office while trying not to alert the others. It is closer to the exit, and she remembers seeing a yellow down by the screen doors.

Shaking with fear and anticipation, the brave woman wanders slowly to the office she found at first. This time, the distance doesn't seem so far, and the walls doesn't feel like they are closing in.

Once Amy reaches the room, there is another notebook sitting on the desk that isn't there when she leaves. It is the same as the others but newer.

Opening it, there is just a note on one of the pages.

Wait for the lone yellow. It will find you. Do not try to take on the others.

You will get hurt, and for that, I am sorry.

Go against your nature this once, and fight. It cannot be helped. This you must do.

There is poison in the bites that cause more pain than just being torn apart. So, if you get bitten, fight the pain and work through it.

Use the knife and get the key.

Find me at the next place. I will be waiting.

De

"OK, that doesn't make me feel better De, but thank you. I will try. Hopefully, you can hear me, and you won't get into much trouble. Not for me."

Looking back at the note, it has vanished. That happens so much in this place.

Gathering her wits, Amy opens the door and sits behind it waiting. Sickness creeps up on her as the stairs creak. A slurping nose sounds. Looking through the crack in the door, Amy takes in the yellow creature. With bulging muscles, this one is terrifying up close. A human face with white eyes and a small head. But the teeth on these ones are the stuff of nightmares. Long, sharp and jagged. Made for piercing and tearing flesh. A small thin nose moves as it sniffs the air. Smelling for what, Amy isn't sure. Can it smell the fear coming from her?

De knows that it is her innocence this particular one is scenting. He made it that way knowing Amy wouldn't survive going up against the others. This way the lone yellow will track her instead, giving her a chance at least. Amy being in this place feels so wrong somehow. He cannot help himself, she needs him, and he will help her often.

The creature is getting closer to Amy now. Her heart is pounding hard in her chest.

A makeshift noose is held in her shaking hands, the knife sitting by her side.

When the Yellow moves into the doorway, Amy acts fast, looping the rope over its head and tying it to the handle. Grabbing the knife, she lunges at the thing. But it laughs at her, actually laughs. Blood dripping from the hideous mouth, Amy notices that her arm has been bitten.

Noticing this she remembers what the note said. But there is no pain. The Yellow tries to step closer, but the rope stops it, making the thing mad. It tears at the rope, and reaches out to Amy, trying to dig its claws into her delicate flesh.

Pain, that's all that Amy feels then. Rushing through her whole body. Panting and sweating she tries to pick up the knife that fell when the pain hit. Her vision is now blurring, and she tries to fight the searing agony that is taking over her body.

De is fighting himself, not being able to stand the pain Amy is going through, yet he is forbidden to stop it. One of his brothers must intervene and hold him down.

"Calm down. She is only a human. What has got into you, Brother?"

"Help her, please," De pleads.

"No! She is nothing to us. It's not like she's yours. Amy isn't one of our kind. Humans are selfish and evil. Let her suffer."

"She isn't like that, not all of them are. I don't understand it, but there is something Brother. I feel strongly for her."

While the brothers have their debate, Amy is fighting the pain. Giving it her all she crawls to the Yellow and stabs him in the foot.

"I'm so sorry." Coming from her before, Amy passes out, and a key falls beside her. The beast no more.

The key is white. A key everyone hopes to find.

On waking, Amy finds herself back in the room of doors. "How?"

"I got you here, Amy."

"De? Hi. Why did you do that? Won't you get in trouble?"

"Yes, I will, but I couldn't leave you like that."

De has convinced his brother to let him take her. She has already endured the pain that the others want.

Amy has rose and hugged De. Warmth engulfs him. The pair stays like that for a while before De realises what he is doing.

"Amy, you must go." Vanishing then and leaving her alone.

"Thank you, De."

The doors around her are all black now, apart from one which is a big white arch shape.

Amy inserts the key, and she is pulled into a very bright room.

Chapter Twenty-Seven

White Room

The light is blinding, but only for a few seconds before it dims revealing a beautiful room.

There is a white table filled with hot food, a white fluffy sofa on one side and a bed with satin sheets on the other. There I also have a set of draws and a fluffy white carpet.

"This room is private Amy, you cannot be watched here, so whatever you do or say cannot be viewed."

"Oh, hi, De, this room is beautiful. What do I need to do here?"

"Nothing. Just wait things out. Rest and have food or sleep. I can get you some books if you like. You are safe now."

"I cannot stay here. My friends might need me."

"Trust me, Amy, they are not thinking about you right now."

"I don't know you. Why should I trust you?"

"Because I like you, Amy. This is not a normal occurrence. We can have fun with humans or procreate, but never fall for one."

"You keep saying human. Are you not one? What are you if you are not human? Alien perhaps?"

De laughs at this. If only she knew what we were.

"No, I am not an alien. What I am will be revealed soon. However, we need to see why I feel connected and protective over you. Who was your father?"

"I do not know. Mother cannot remember him. Every time she tries her headaches. She hasn't had any other partners, just him and my dad. I must look like him because my mum has brown eyes and fair hair."

"That is interesting. If you have our blood in you, that will explain a lot. It would also make this journey you are on void, and we would have to apologise. I must investigate this, Amy. Rest and enjoy the books." Before leaving, De places a kiss on Amy's head, which she likes, very much.

Men do not interest her usually, nor females. Benny tries, but there is no attraction. Maybe she is different.

Sitting on the fluffy sofa Amy looks through the books that De left, deciding on a thriller to pass the time. The food looks good, but she cannot bring herself to eat after seeing all the carnage.

Maybe a thriller isn't such a good idea.

After reading a few chapters, Amy decides to check the place out. There aren't any doors, not even a toilet. All this time she hasn't needed to pee, yet she has had plenty of water and food.

The draws in the room have nothing in them. More books sit on top, there is also a crossword book and some sudoku puzzles with a few pencils.

The food is still hot, there is pasta with cheese. Vegetables and potatoes. Some fish, wine, and hot chocolate. Warm jam roly-poly with custard. Bread rolls with butter. It is a feast of things she loves. Deciding that she needs to eat, Amy takes the roly-poly to the sofa and carries on with her book.

Meanwhile, De is trying to search through the memories. There is nothing in Amy's. He needs permission to investigate anyone else's past.

Knowing that time is limited, De asks the higher-ups for permission. If Amy is one of them, they need to know.

His requests are granted.

The past tells him everything he needs to know. They have made a huge mistake.

De has a lot to tell everyone. They will not be pleased.

Although he is happy that she will not suffer anymore. His feelings are warranted and true. De has found his match.

Chapter Twenty-Eight

Fixing It

Amy has been sitting and reading for a long time. Occasionally getting up to drink, or just stretch her legs.

"Can I leave now please?"

De appears then. He looks happy, but worried.

"Amy, I have news. You cannot know it all yet. However, I can do this." He kisses her. Amy is shocked but leans in and accepts him.

De pulls back and looks down at her. A beautiful smile spread across his face.

"Wow, um. De?" Amy tries to talk, but the words don't come out.

"You have our blood, Amy. It is a long story. One I cannot tell you yet. We are so sorry that you have gone through this, you should have gone elsewhere. I will make it up to you. There will be a decision that you can make at the end. All will be revealed, I promise as your match."

"Match?"

"Oh, we are meant to be. You will see. Right now, be patient and come with me. Your friends await." In a flash of light, they appear in a different room. There is a man sitting by a desk. Dark hair like De, but his eyes are solid silver, he is scary.

"How lovely to meet you in person Amy. We have so much to talk about."

"You are the one who spoke in the first room."

"Why yes, that was me. If I had known who you were, that would never have happened. You would have been welcomed, and your father contacted to guide you. Things have changed now, however. When your friends arrive, decisions will be made. Until then sweet child, tell me, how did you find my little game?"

"Terrifying."

"Good, good. That's what I wanted to hear. You had an easy one, my dear. Most are so much worse."

Amy paled at his words, realising that her friends must be going through hell right now, or they have been.

"Are my friends, OK?"

"Of course. They are resilient. Well, Julie and Duke. Their fates are sealed now, we are awaiting Benny. He was a tricky one I must say. Do you want to watch the rest of his journey?"

"No, thank you. I will wait."

"OK, I understand. Take Amy to a waiting room. Spend time with your match."

De takes Amy's hand and leads her to a silver door. They enter to find comfy silver sofas and a TV.

"Do you want to watch the outside world for a bit? Or I can find a human film?"

"Human film, as you say, will be good, thanks. Something funny."

"Angry birds?"

"Yeah, that sounds good."

As the couple bond over a silly cartoon, a mistake needs fixing. Amy's father is powerful. If he knows what was done to his only child, there will be hell to pay.

A dead one tasted her blood, luckily it will not reform. If it wasn't for her guide things would have been so much worse.

Amy will be able to choose her fate. Not like the others. When she finds out her heritage, things are going to get messy.

There is a lot of grovelling to do and treats to give. Luckily, Amy has a huge heart.

Chapter Twenty-Nine
Room Ten, Benny's Journey

The reception lounge is quiet, Benny awaits his turn.

"OK, Benny, Which room would u like."

Looking at the remaining keys, he chooses a plain black one.

"OK, that one is rarely picked. Our last guide will take you."

Another beautiful female takes his bags. She has the same eyes and hair; however, there was no smile or polite hello. This lady was very sour.

"This way." That is all she says to Benny. Following her to where he needs to be, his thoughts go to different places.

Before he knew it, they were at a black door. The lady opened it and took in the bags she carried. Benny followed.

"How did I get here so quickly? Why can I not remember how I got here?"

"I am your guard or guide. However, you want to see it. You will know when the time comes. I don't want to waste time talking to you." She was gone then, leaving Benny in a dark room.

He saw a bed with black satin sheets. Sitting down he waited.

"Benny, at long last. You are my final person. Please make yourself comfortable."

"Great, an eery voice in a dark room, how exciting."

"Yes, well. We all have our hobbies, don't we, Benny?"

"What do you want with me?"

"Now where is that sweet teddy bear everyone sees?"

"He isn't here at the moment. Just get on with it. I am determined to get Amy on this trip, this is holding me up."

"So impatient, aren't we? I must give you something before we start. Whatever I show you will not have an effect, will it? You are a psychopath. You have no conscience or emotions. My gift to you is feelings. You will know everything that you've done and see it through new eyes. Taking this path of yours with full knowledge of what you are doing."

Benny does not like the sound of that.

When the emotions hit, the pain is intense.

"Give it a minute to settle. Then we will start."

This time there is no recording playing on a wall. Benny is thrown into the memories. As if he was there again.

The first is in a field, he is playing catch with a small girl. Benny was about four, and it was the time he realised his problem.

The small girl has curly red hair and freckles and hazel eyes and a pale complexion. Benny hits her little nose with the ball. It is an accident, but he sees the blood and feels nothing. He keeps hitting her with the ball to try and feel something. The poor thing lies on the floor screaming in pain. Benny just looks at the blood on his hands from the ball and walks away.

There are no consequences for his actions that day. The girl doesn't tell her parents what happens. Benny learns then to pretend he has emotions and acts like a sweet child in front of others. In private, he does everything he can to try and feel something, anything.

The next memory is Benny in class. He has many friends that he can manipulate. One girl will not give him attention, so he makes sure the class only gives her negative encounters. They will tease her endlessly.

Benny pretends to be the only one that cared while convincing the others to hurt her. It makes her finally pay attention to him.

She is beautiful, with bright blue eyes and long golden blond hair.

If it isn't for Benny, she would have been very popular. He makes up stories that her parents are claiming benefits that they don't need and steal from people. He isn't questioned about it, as nobody but him knows her. And that's how he wants it to stay.

Her parents has good jobs. Her father is a solicitor, and her mother a nurse at the local doctor's. Yet everyone believes Benny's manipulations. At the age of ten, this is easily done.

Benny going through this with a conscience is hell for him. Feeling everything that he should have.

This is only the beginning, Benny.

Next, he is standing in a field. The same girl is sitting by his side while he looks around. Getting down with the golden-haired beauty, he wraps his arm around her. They are around fourteen here. Benny is acting like the sweet man, but he really isn't.

Knowing what is coming, the present Benny tries to pull himself away. But he is stuck in the memory and has to go along with it.

"Please, I know what is going to happen. I cannot see this. It wasn't my fault that my feelings were flawed. I have them now, and I regret everything I've ever done." Benny screams in his head. The memory then pauses.

"There are too many things to show you. Your evil deeds are vast. Yes, you couldn't help not having feelings, but you know what was wrong and right. So watch and feel."

The memory starts again then.

Benny reaches around the sweet girl. He kisses her. She lets him. It is her first kiss, which she had saved just for him. Her so-called saviour.

The kiss isn't enough for Benny. He wants all of her, and he refuses to wait.

"I am not ready for that," she gently tells Benny.

"You are mine. Nobody else is allowed to have you like this. So I am taking what I'm due. All these years I've protected this body of yours."

She tries to get up and leave then, not liking the way the date is going.

"If you love me, then you can wait. You will be my first when I am old enough and ready," she pleads.

"It isn't a matter of love babe. You owe me. Now come here before I stop protecting you from all the boys who want to take advantage and the girls who would beat you."

Benny then takes what he wants. The sweet girl cries as he takes her innocence. He then leaves her there, lying in her own blood.

Rumours then flies around the school about her giving Benny her body. He claims her as his, but that doesn't stop the catcalls and the bitchy comments.

After that day, her life becomes unbearable. Benny is cold towards her yet takes her when he feels the need.

Five months later, the poor girl finds out she is pregnant. Taking her own life then. Telling her parents that she is pregnant at fourteen and seeing all the faces of those who hate her, would have been too much. Four years of ridicule and beatings is enough.

Benny just go on with his life. Finding other girls to get pleasure from. The only thing he could feel.

The present Benny is crying now remembering her sweet face and gentleness.

"What the hell did I do? She was amazing. Please make it stop now. I will take whatever punishment I'm due. Just don't show me anymore."

With him only just knowing feelings, it is all hitting harder than it should. His pain is evident.

"Get used to having feelings Benny, they are not going anywhere now you have them." Sobbing hard he is put in another memory.

Benny is sixteen and works part-time at the hospital where his dad resides. He assists with small duties, moving chairs and trolleys around the hospital amongst other things. Being a renowned doctor, you would think his father would figure out the problems Benny had. But the man is always too busy, never noticing what his son does. Also, Benny is smart and hides the darkness within. His mum loves him so much that she ignores anything that should have been concerning.

Being at the hospital, Benny has a lot of ways he can do wrong. Mostly he switches meds when nurses have their backs turned. Just to see what would happen.

A lot of nurses get in trouble, some even losing their jobs.

Getting bored with that, he tries different things. Turning off machines that provided oxygen to patients. He doesn't do it often, mostly doing things at parts of the hospital that he isn't working in.

Things get worse as time goes on. Patients who are really sick start dying. Benny isn't allowed in those parts of the hospital due to his age. However, that doesn't stop him. He is fascinated with how easy it is to make the thermally ill residents stop breathing.

A little too much morphine or a pillow over their faces.

This goes on for weeks but stops, so nobody will suspect him.

Another thing is selling stolen medication to drug dealers. Benny wants fast cash, hoping that will give him things to make his life better. Wanting the best of everything, even at a young age.

This carries on all through his teen years. He has money from different sources. People are easily manipulated by him. Elderly women will leave him cash before they pass or properties. Working at the hospital has many benefits.

That goes on until Benny has attended university and met Amy. He wants her then. But she can't be manipulated. It makes him want her more. So he becomes a good friend to her. Or so she thinks.

He never lets anyone get close, which is hard considering everyone who meets her is drawn to the amazing woman. That is until Julie and Duke. The four become fast friends, even if Benny hates Amy not giving him her undivided attention.

His acquaintance Drake has a thing for Julie, which has many advantages. That is until things go really wrong. Not for Benny, he relishes in the chaos.

Julie gets drunk a lot then, and he is able to satisfy the craving he has for Amy, by taking her friend when the need calls. Duke never knows, and neither does Amy. Benny willn't allow it. Acting like a best friend to Duke.

A few drops of medication in Julie's drinks help them get what he wants without Julie knowing it is him sleeping with her.

All these memories play out, and Benny is breaking. These things are just the tip of the iceberg. From the age of four, his deeds get worse.

He can't have a pet; they always disappeared. He pretends to be heartbroken each time.

The neighbour's one-year-old son ends up on the road in his pushchair. His mum has to convince the child's parents that Benny isn't anywhere near the baby.

Benny wants to see what will happen to a baby if it is hit by a car. Not admitting it to his mother but telling her that he doesn't know how the chair gets there. Some kids are playing nearby is his story.

The baby is only left for a second while the mum is getting her shopping out of the car. Luckily, the road is quiet.

Benny is pushed into the worst memory then. One that will really break him.

"Tell me what you feel when the knife enters your stomach, I need details. Not just that it hurts, but the actual emotions that come with each wound."

Benny is working with a gang. He was great at getting information, even at a young age. There are benefits of having no morals or a conscience.

The woman he is torturing has already told him what he wants to know. But he is curious about feelings, so he uses this time to experiment.

"Tell me!"

"Fear, dread and pain."

"No, I want details. How the metal feels when it enters. What the blood feels like as it is released. How your heart feels as it pumps blood toward the wound. Every detail." This goes on until she passes out, unable to give him what he craves.

The woman is the gang member's wife and innocent, but Benny knows that. The information he gets proves her to be. The gang thinks she is informing their rivals as she is near their territory. Unbeknownst to them, it is the doctors that she has gone to. Not wanting her husband to know, the woman decides to see a different doctor than usual. Wanting to surprise the man she loves with her whole heart.

Knowing that he can't get what he wants. Benny calls for the woman's husband. Telling him that there is nothing he can get out of her.

They trust him to do things without anyone else there, so none of the members knows the truth.

A gunshot echoes through the room as the husband puts a bullet in his wife's head. Blinking back tears as he walks out of the room, not wanting to show weakness to the other members.

Later, when he finds out the truth, the man shoots himself. The guilt has destroyed him.

It is an informant from the other gang who has told him that the wife has never spoken to any of them. But she is seen entering the doctor's surgery.

His girlfriend is the receptionist, who manages to get the information that his wife is with the child.

"Well, Benny. I think that is enough of going down memory lane. Your Path starts now. The journey that follows will be very painful. Your guard or guide, she will be around when the needs are a must."

All the lights go out then, and a tearful Benny is left standing by another black door with a blue glow coming from the edges.

"Take this." The Grumpy woman is suddenly by his side. She hands him a water bottle, then disappears.

Taking hold of the handle, Benny opens the door. Blue light surrounds him as he walks through it.

Chapter Thirty

Harder When You Feel

The blue light that surrounds Benny dims to reveal a cave. It is now dark with just a small lamp that illuminates part of the path heading further into the depths.

Taking the lamp from the wall. A shaking Benny decides to head into the darkness. Not liking the feeling of fear.

Each step is harder for him, Darkness and tight spaces have never been an issue before. Now it is hitting him how much he needs to face.

"I deserve all that is coming to me." He keeps saying to himself.

The guard observes him. Her hatred for this type of human is pouring from her. She does not feel an ounce of pity and wonders why she was tasked with this one.

Meanwhile, the path that Benny is on gets thinner as it descends. There are things crawling along the walls now, reminding him of all the poor creatures he tortured, just to see the turmoil in them that he could not feel. He isn't really trying to kill anything, but that often happens.

When he gets deep into the cave system, there is another lamp. This one has a purple glow. Around it fly these bat-like creatures. Black with purple transparent wings. Benny can't see them well until one flies right towards him. They has human-like faces, with wide purple eyes and long black teeth. Claws descending from the long wings. Short legs with long silver talons being attached. When the first one sees Benny, it lets out a screech, alerting the other to his presence.

All then start flying around his head. Scaring him as each scratches his face with the talons and claws.

With Benny only starting to get used to having feelings, his legs buckle in fear. Sweat dripping from his brow into the scratches that now litter his face. He starts to crawl along the path, trying to get away from them. But they descend on his body. Their claws are razor sharp. They detach his ears from his head then, like he used to do to the rodents he found.

Screaming in pain, he tries to shoo them away. But they just grab his hands and take off some fingers. More come towards him, taking different parts of him. His nose has been torn off along with his lips. He tries to cover his jewels, but they see this, and each one looks as if they are smiling.

Loud screams come from his bloody mouth as they rib off his private parts.

He does this to one of the men he has tortured once. Again, after the man has given him the information he wants.

When the pain becomes too much, Benny passes out in a pool of blood.

The creatures leave then and disappear into the purple light.

After several hours, Benny wakes. He screams and feels his body. Everything is back in place, but the memory of the pain is still at the forefront of his mind.

A phantom pain coming from his nether region. That is one pain he will never forget.

Scars litter his body in places. He can feel the raised bumps.

Looking around now he finds his water and drinks. Getting slowly torn apart is thirsty work. There is also an apple, for which he is thankful.

His guard only has left him the minimum of supplies.

After eating, Benny reluctantly stands, retrieving the lamp from the floor. The path looking even more daunting now. Slowly, he starts his journey again.

Maybe the worst of this is over? No, it is not.

Another light glows ahead, and this terrifies Benny. Yellow is what shines brightly. As he gets closer, however, there is nothing around it. His relief is short-lived, though, as a figure appears beside the lamp. The golden-haired beauty is standing there holding a baby in her arms. Blood coats her sleeves coming from the cuts that took her life. Benny can now see the baby's face; it looks just like him. Light blue, almost grey eyes look right at him. Small tufts of dark blond hair peeks from the black blanket that is wrapped around the child.

"Do you want to hold him?" she asks.

Benny reaches out towards the child. His heart pounding hard. He feels something. It is a powerful emotion. Guessing that it is guilt. What else could it be?

Just as Benny is about to hold the beautiful child, there is a flash of light. In his arms lay the blanket covered in blood, it is now the blanket he used to sit on in that field where the child was conceived. Sadness, that is what he now feels, immense sadness.

"These hurt so much. Take them back, please."

The begging remains unanswered. Benny is left to his pain and thoughts.

This man is breaking already. With emotions, he really does have a heart of gold. After hours of crying, he falls into a deep slumber. As he sleeps the cave around him changes, his next task awaiting him.

Chapter Thirty-One

Going On

Red and swollen eyes look up to see a beautiful blue sky. Benny panics and looks around. Confusion evident.

"Where is the cave?" he asks himself, but a female answers his question.

"You are at the next step. Now being familiar with some of your emotions, this can continue."

"OK. Thank you. What happens now?"

"Do not thank me. This is my job, and I will never make things easy for you. Whether you can feel it now or not, it doesn't matter to me. Here are some supplies, again do not thank me, I must feed you." She then throws a bag at him.

"Oh. Well, I appreciate it anyway. What do I call you?"

"Nothing. You will never know my name. Guard will suffice as I don't plan on guiding you much. No pet names or anything else. Just guard." She then turns and walks, slowly fading away with each step taken.

There aren't many opinions for him now. He is in an open field of grass and flowers. Looking beautiful and not threatening at all.

Getting to his feet, Benny starts to walk. At first, there is a pleasant smell from the flowers, a gentle heat from the sunshine, and grass which glitters in the light.

Nothing bad is expected to come from this place but looks can be deceiving as Benny has proven many times.

All at once, the flowers start to squirt a liquid from their blossoms. Most of it hits Benny's bare arms. A burning sensation occurs, and his arms start to blister. He tries to brush off the black liquid, but it pulls his skin off with each wipe. Trying to run now, with nowhere to hide, just thousands of flowers around spitting tar, unable to escape the pain he drops onto a patch of grass.

The burning stops, and the pain eases. For a minute, he feels safe. Seeing that the flowers are still Benny takes a drink and assesses the situation. The tar-like substance has gone from his arms.

He realises that staying on the grass is best. Taking in the red marks on his body, Benny notices that his clothes are different now. He is in black shorts and a tight black vest top with silver and black trainers as footwear.

Each patch of grass has different coloured flowers between them. In the distance is a black path. The flowers that burnt his body are dark purple in colour. Red and black flowers sit between him and the next patch of grass. Determined now Benny gets up, secures the bag of supplies, and runs with everything he has.

When his feet hit the petals, they shred through the trainers. The black leaves dripping with blood. Looking closely there are body parts that have been pierced by the leaves and left to rot. Almost like souvenirs.

The petals do not cut his skin, only the material of his footwear. When his feet are bare that is when the black stems try to grab him. The sharp barbs digs into his soft flesh and muscle, trying to get Benny to fall.

One of the stems has taken a toe and placed it on one of the barbs. Benny falls then and the red petals start to rip his shorts and t-shirt. Crawling the rest of the way, he makes it to the next safe place. The flowers again look still, and normal.

Catching his breath and replenishing himself while his body starts to heal. The ripped clothes are now whole again.

It doesn't take long until everything but the toe has been fixed.

"What, I don't get my toe back? It is a good job it wasn't my junk," he shouts out, trying to a joke while his heart is slamming against his chest in fear. It seems to be a popular emotion for him.

The next lot of flowers look beautiful. Pink and silver petals with silver stems. But he knows now not to trust something so beautiful.

Standing now, and getting ready to run, Benny spots someone on the path that he is heading towards. They look female, or a man with long red hair. He knows that this person must know how to get to the next place. With that in mind, Benny heads in that direction.

This bed of flowers is different. They are really soft and cool to the touch, which slows down the running and makes Benny look closer. Each one is unique, with different patterns on the petals. The man cannot help but admire them, touching each detail with delicate hands. He remains with them for a long time, unable to stop himself.

Hours go by, with no attempt to move. Benny doesn't notice the skeletons littering the ground under the plants. He likes this emotion, all is peaceful. Yet there is a memory that surfaces. One of the bloody blankets in his arms, a baby that could have been. Shaking his head as a stronger emotion hit. Grief, raw and overpowering.

Getting himself up fast, he runs again, not looking at the flowers. Reaching the grass patch, Benny looks back and sees that the flowers are not beautiful at all. There is a silver and pink mist that must make you obsessed. Brown weeds are all that is there now under the mist, along with the dead.

The path is right up ahead. There is no longer a person standing there waiting for him. One more set of flowers left before the destination. Bright yellow with black stems.

"What are you going to do to me now, little flowers." These are the last words spoken before Benny takes off running again.

He should not have run. His feet stick to these ones, making him fall into the others. Unable to move now or speak. With no options at all now, Benny decides to give up. A tear falls onto the sticky goo. As soon as the salty water touches the petal of one flower, Benny is released. Sadness is what he feels, and it has set him free. Not thinking too much about it, Benny rises to his feet and jumps the small distance to the path. Surprising himself with the distance he made before getting stuck.

Dropping to the solid earth and kissing the warm ground before collapsing altogether. This man passes out a lot.

Chapter Thirty-Two

Black Path

After passing out, Benny has slept for a good half hour.

"Again? Really." The guard appears, staring down at his sleepy form.

"Sorry, I am not used to all these feelings. They seem to be taking a toll. And those plants were evil."

"They were just doing their jobs, as am I. So, get up, you have a long way to go."

"Yes, I understand. I'm up," he tells her before rising and standing before her.

"Good. Here is an energy bar. It might stop you fainting long enough to get you a little further."

"Thank you."

"My job, remember."

This time the guard just vanishes before he can ask anything. So taking a big bite of his bar Benny starts to walk the black path, leading out off the field. There are many flowers scattered around, but the path itself looks to be clear.

Will they never learn?

Benny walks the path for quite a while, without spotting anything but flowers and fields of grass. Not wanting to give up, or take a break, just hoping that the end is close. Something else that is a new experience. Having hope.

Getting tired, the hopeful man sits and takes a well-needed break. He walks for nearly a day if you count the hours. The sun not moving in this place.

As Benny is sitting and having some water, the redhead finds him. The person is a female and doesn't look happy. She is holding a book or maybe a diary. Walking towards him with a determined look on her pretty face.

He knows this woman. She is the girl that was hurt by his hands when he was small. Benny's heart hurts, this woman is beyond beautiful. Milky white skin, dark red curls that fall to the middle of her back, a few freckles over her tiny nose and eyes that are big and shining bright, a stunning hazel colour that is filled with hatred. A white dress covers her tiny frame, her feet bare, with black nail polish on her toes and fingernails.

Benny remembers what he did to her, and his heart breaks a little more. That young girl was so sweet and kind. Feeling hatred now, but at himself, not the beauty in front of him.

"I am so sorry, so so sorry. That man is no more, and I will never let him hurt another soul. That I promise."

The woman says nothing back. Her eyes are focused on him still though, unsure whether to believe the man before her.

The book in her hand is then placed in front of Benny. The woman then steps back into the field. Turning into a puddle of red, she vanishes.

When the shock has worn off, he picks up the book. It looks to be a photo album. The pictures show many different views of the path he is on, which doesn't help at all. That is until one of the pictures falls out. The path then splits in two. The black rubble one he was on is still there along with a smooth black path that has appeared. Deciding to try the new direction, Benny walks the new way.

As he walks Benny looks at the other pictures. Each one change the further along he gets. Finally, there is something different, a crack. This one is ageing now, so Benny drops another picture. One that shows a bridge. It is the one that looks promising. The others are still changing, but the bridge stays on that image. As soon as the picture hits the floor a bridge forms, yet the path stays where it is. Benny drops another picture, one that has changed to an image of a river.

As it hits the bridge a river forms underneath, there is then a picture of a boat. Benny gets the message now and places the boat picture in the water. He is instantly transported into the moving boat, which has nothing to steer it or make it stop. Thinking that this is a bad idea, Benny tries to get out. The boat however speeds up, taking him on a wild ride.

Excitement floods Benny's system, and he feels the adrenaline pumping through his veins. Another new feeling, one he isn't sure about. Yet when the boat slows down, stopping at a door, Benny realises that he had fun. If all feelings were like this, then he welcomes them.

Reaching out to pull himself up onto the bank, he nearly falls into the water. Managing to finally get to the door, Benny finds that it is locked. Made of solid black wood there is no way he can break it. An idea suddenly hits him. The book. Opening it to see a picture of a key, a smile forms, giving the feeling of happiness and pride.

After dropping the picture on the floor though, nothing happens. Benny tries this several more times before deciding that it will not produce a key. Angry at himself he slams his hand on the door. That hand is holding the picture. Which in turn makes it open wide.

"I am an idiot. Of course, it wouldn't work on the floor." After berating himself, the sulking man takes a big step through the doorway.

Chapter Thirty-Three

Onward and Downwards

Stepping through the large doorway, Benny feels relieved.

He thinks that the worst is over.

This room is long and narrow. Each wall is a different shade of grey; the door has turned into another wall shutting Benny in. There is only one way to go, so that is where he went. Following a corridor that leads off one side of the room he walks. Walking the hall, he notices that the floor starts to slope. It isn't steep, but there is a definite drop.

The walls start to gain colour the further he goes. Starting from dark blues and purple.

When Benny reaches a lilac wall, he realises that it is wet. His hand is covered in lilac paint. The floor then becomes slippery with white paint and slopes even more, causing him to fall and slide into a waiting room. He drops down to another floor, falling through the first room and continuing to fall until he was four floors below.

Landing with a thud, Benny hits a solid metal base. The floors above him seem to be melting and merging into various colours, dripping down around him. Filling up the metal room that seemed to have no exit. Soon he will not be able to move, the liquid falling being so thick and heavy. There is nowhere to go, nothing that will help him get out, or stop the falling, melting death trap.

The room starts to heat up as it fills. A memory comes to Benny then. A plastic house. He wants to see what will happen if a living thing is inside and lights on fire. One of his friends has a purple playhouse. She always has friends around. It is quite large. There are four layers to it.

Two girls are in the top tier when Benny decides to experiment. He sets fire to the house using lighter fluid and string to keep it lit. The girls fell through the layers, screaming as they did. One of the parents runs over and tries to get them out. The melted plastic sticks to her hands as she reaches for them.

When they are finally pulled out, their bodies are covered in melted plastic and blood. Blisters also cover their arms and faces.

When the girls are taken to the hospital, Benny is questioned. He is only six, so everyone believes him when he says there are some older boys playing with fire. That he fears them, so he has ran home.

His mum can't verify that as she is asleep from a long shift. His dad is in his office doing some work. They thinks Benny is watching TV. So that is what Benny's dad has told the police. His son has come back and has been watching TV.

As Benny reminisces about those poor girls, the room keeps filling. There isn't going to be anyone to save him. When the liquid reaches his calves, the burning gets worse. The melted plastic sticking to his skin. Lumps of metal that are holding the structure together now fell, red-hot and sharp, digging into Benny's shoulders and arms. Tears of pain and fear run down his sweat-soaked face, while his screams fill the room.

Finally, the room stops filling. Benny is covered in blood. His hair is gone, and that beautiful face of his is filled with blisters and cuts. His appearance is unrecognisable. This time he does not faint, taking the pain that he thinks is deserved. The revelation saves him from more pain.

Slowly, a mist fills the space, knocking the blood-soaked man out. Each breath he takes is painful due to fumes that damage his lungs.

Screaming as he wakes up, Benny takes in his surroundings. The metal prison is now gone and a wooden room taking its place. It looks to be a cabin of sorts, or maybe a shed.

The pain that wrecks Benny's body is now a dull ache, but the memory is still clear. Especially the one of the girls as they were taken in an ambulance. Their bodies are forever altered.

Benny looks at his body. There are scars all over it now, but his hair is back, the metal and plastic no more. His internal scars will also stay.

This place holds nothing, a bottle of water by his side along with the bag of supplies. Taking a sip of water, he sits for a while. That big brain of his trying to make sense of everything that he has done. Breaking more and more as all those new emotions bombard him. Tears now streaming and sobs escaping him.

The guard looks at him sitting there. She cannot hate this human as much now. He really is sorry for the past. The deeds cannot be forgiven, but maybe they can make him try to be better now.

Realising now why she was tasked with this one.

Appearing by his side and being a little nicer, the guard speaks, "The path isn't much longer, bear with it. You are doing well."

"Are you actually being a little kind to me? Is this feeling gratitude?"

"It may well be. Don't think I like you, me not being so harsh is not anything. We are better than humans so hate doesn't control us."

"What are you if not human?"

"Enough Questions. Eat this food and your task shall start soon enough." A package is then thrown towards Benny containing real food.

"Thank you, guard."

With that, she disappears with a small smile on her face, which only lasts a second.

Benny opens the package. There are strawberries with ice cream, a pasta salad, cold meats, chicken bits and crisps. There is also a cup of hot, milky tea. He starts to eat. Taking a sip of his tea, relishing the flavour for the first time. Never really tasting it before as he couldn't enjoy it.

Taking a bite of the strawberries with ice cream, Benny lets out a little moan, never did he think that food could make him feel like this. Happiness flows through him, all this time he had no idea what having feelings could be like. That was until he remembered the bad again.

The happiness short-lived.

Leaving the rest of it, he leans back on the wooden surface, closing his eyes and thinking about all he has done. Horror at who he became, hating his past self.

Shaking and sobbing, Benny couldn't bring himself to move. Crippling sadness takes over.

"He is broken," the guard tells the ones watching.

"We will not get much out of him now. All the planned tasks will be useless. His regret is stronger than we thought it would be. That heart is bigger than expected. The person he pretends to be is who he wanted to be deep down. So what do we do now?"

"We make him take responsibility for all the evil he has done. He will make amends. Whether it be here or out there. One way or another he must pay."

"So we are all decided? Benny is to finish here, but the journey he is on shall continue elsewhere?"

"Yes, we are decided," the watching ones all speak up.

The guard appears again then next to a broken Benny. His sobs do not let up.

Touching one of his shaking shoulders, the guard gets his attention.

"You cannot finish your path here. So we have an idea. Come, we are going now."

Benny just looks up at her with red eyes and is unable to speak through his sobs.

Taking his arm, the guard gets them away from the wooden room.

Chapter Thirty-Four

Results Are In

Benny is taken to a room that looks like an office. Chairs are scattered around. There is a man at the desk with silver eyes.

"Sit, Benny." His voice sounds familiar.

"Your acquaintances will be along shortly."

Benny remains quiet. He sits and awaits whatever is coming.

The door opens then, and Julie walks through. She is pale and looks tired, her usually bright eyes are dull. Scars litter her body that can be seen. Julie takes in Benny's appearance.

"I am so sorry, Julie, for what I did to you all those times." Benny managed to get out.

"What are you talking about, Benny? You did nothing to me."

"I took advantage of you, several times. Drugging you and sleeping with you. I will never forgive my actions."

Julie is stunned, not knowing what to say. She just sits. Then tells him, "I don't remember anything, so why tell me? Now I will think about it. Thanks for that." Benny wasn't expecting that, he thought she would shout or argue. But she is indifferent.

The man smiles at them, taking in the conversation between the two.

Again, the door opens, and Duke walks in. He looks at everyone and nods. Scars also litter his body.

Benny notices then that they are all back in their original clothes.

Duke looks at Benny, "You look like crap, mate. I've never seen you upset over anything. Is Amy, OK?"

Benny just shrugs, not looking at Duke knowing what he did to Julie. Duke had always wanted her, and Benny betrayed his friend in the worst way possible.

"Benny, what is it?" Duke asks again.

"Enough!" The silver-eyed man states. His aura is so strong that it makes everyone take notice.

At that moment, Amy walks through the door with a guide by her side. Benny looks over to her. He takes in her beauty for the first time with feelings. His heart pounds fast, and love fills him. He is about to go and hug her when the guide pushes her behind him. Looking at Benny with hatred and warning.

"You will not touch my love." The guard warns Benny. Amy touches the man's arm.

"De, don't. Please. He is my friend."

"He is not your friend, Amy. This man is nobody's friend."

Benny feels anger then as he sees De take Amy by the hand, and for her to look at him with love.

"Amy? Who is this De person?" Benny asks.

"He is the man I love, Benny. We are together."

"Love? We only just got here. How can you be in love?"

"We have been here longer than you think Benny. I am sorry but there is nobody for me but De. You and I could never have been anything. I cannot explain why."

Earlier Between Amy and De

Amy sits in the room she is given, boredom setting in again. That is until De decides to pay a visit.

"Hello, Amy. I have been sent to explain things. Only you can know what I'm about to disclose."

"OK, De, shoot."

"Daniel, that is my name. But tell no one. That is a must. Our names hold power. When we are out of this room, call me De."

"Not a problem, Daniel." His name on her lips is everything, but he needs to tell her everything.

"Right, well here goes. We each have a match, someone that is perfect for us. So that we can reproduce. We are instantly attracted to that person, however feelings do not come until they spend time together. Not all our kind are compatible with each other, which is why some take a human just to have a child. We cannot fall for someone who is not our match, although we can have fun, love will never form."

Amy listens, earnestly. Smiling at what Daniel tells her.

"Your father Amy is a powerful man. He is one of the first. We have different jobs; our family takes on this task. Your father's family are higher up. He has never reproduced, a match never found. Your existence has only just reached us. He has always known and wants you to have a long human life before being part of our world. A meeting has been

164

arranged, and he will see you. Wanting to know you. Watching all your accomplishments made him really proud."

"He is proud. Well, that is nice. But having him around occasionally would have been better."

"That would not have been possible. Your mother was not allowed to remember him. Her memories had to be cleared of anything to do with your father. I am sorry Amy, he had no choice. Your stepdad is a good man, he was chosen to bring you up and love your mother. Only the best to be in your life. That man had no idea, he was just put in the path of you both. The love he has is genuine."

"That is good I suppose. Carry on, Daniel."

"Right, OK."

Daniel carries on with the way of our world. He explains how everyone ended up here. What will happen to everyone, and what does this mean for both of them?

Which cannot be revealed yet.

The pair spend time talking and getting to know each other. Falling harder each moment.

Present

Getting back to the results. The group are waiting now. Benny still throwing daggers at De, who now has Amy sitting on his lap.

The silver-eyed man gets up and walks over to them. The guides/guards are suddenly present, standing by the one they accompanied.

"Now you all need to listen carefully to what I am telling you. Do not interrupt, just listen. When you leave here the memories of this place will fade, but not the lessons." Each of

165

the group wants to talk, but they are unable to. Except for Amy, she already knows this part.

"When you left to travel, your destiny was sealed. A journey would inevitably lead you here. Amy is the exception. I will not leave you wondering anymore."

"On the way here, there was an accident. I pulled you out before the collision. You were bought here to decide what happens to you. Will you be able to have a chance, and where you will head if you don't survive?"

"You see, we are Angels of death. There are way too many humans to only have one of us, so we reproduced. With many families all over the world now. The guides are my family. Scarlette my wife is a fallen, but my match. My sons and daughters are by your side. Julie, I believe you met my youngest. That sneaky child wanted you to finish first to win a bet. I apologise for that."

Julie just nods, unable to say anything.

"It was also a test, as I know what she was planning. One you failed miserably. You have all been judged and a decision has been made on your fate."

Chapter Thirty-Five

Julie's Fate

"Julie, I will start with you."

Standing up, she walks over to death not knowing how she got up and moved.

When she reaches the desk, death sits, taking out a screen. Looking over it before looking back to Julie.

"You failed. Simple really. You only do things that benefit your. Even when you help someone, it is because the end result makes things better for you. Even when Benny told you what he did, you decided not to acknowledge it, as the thought would make things difficult in your life. I have taken in everything from the past and what you have done here."

"We have all decided that you should die from the accident, and your soul will remain on this plane until you can learn to be selfless. Working on the paths, suffering as the others do. That is the rest of your journey. All our seniors have viewed the footage, and all are in agreement. Now you may speak."

"I am not selfish. So all that was for nothing? This should not happen to me. Amy got a hot man out of this. My mother made me this way. Punish her."

"The decision is made. Not sit while the others hear their results."

Julie tries to say more but her body will not respond.

Duke's Fate

Duke looks at Julie, hating that he thought she was special. Now seeing her for what she really is.

"Next, I shall reveal Duke's fate. Come here, young man."

Again, the body doing as death asks of it.

"Duke, now you were very difficult. You are beyond kind. That showed through all the bad. The past you had has made things difficult, yet you remain good in many ways. So we have decided that you will die in the accident."

"What! No please I have loads I want to do." Duke is surprised that he can talk.

"That isn't the end dear child. Because you went through so much, we have all come to the same conclusion. A rebirth. You will have a second chance at life, and we will be watching you, if you come out the same, then this shall be revisited, and you will be held accountable. You will have good parents this time. A chance to be the person you want to be without all the hardships. Good luck."

Duke has tears in his eyes as he walks back to the seat and plonks himself down, taking in the words that death said.

He can live his life again. A good life, but he'll die in this one. He was happy with that.

Benny's Fate

"Now, Benny. You are a strange one. Even my eldest daughter started to feel sorry for you, and she is a very tough one. come here."

Benny does as he is told.

"Look at you. Having feelings has messed you up, haven't they? Well, your companions should hear that you were a psychopath. He had no emotions, so we gave him them, to allow him an understanding of his fast actions."

Gasps are heard from the others. Shocked at the information.

"We felt that the best option for you is being able to make amends for your past, by surviving the accident and keeping your emotions. Allowing you to now feel. People will see that you had a bad head injury, explaining the change in character. This is a punishment and a chance to redeem yourself. Be better."

All Benny can do is nod in agreement. Julie tries hard to add her opinion, but her mouth remains closed. Only grunts coming from her.

"Julie, our decisions are final, so please stop trying to change our minds."

Amy's Fate

"Now, Amy. You can remain with De for the moment. Your case is different. We have spoken with your father and agreed to your fate. Amy is half angel. Her father is the first angel of death. He will teach you our ways, Amy. But not yet. Your human life will continue, and at the end of it, you will return. Your father wants you to have that life."

"No, I don't want to lose De. I cannot leave him now," she pleads.

"I cannot lose her either. You know what this will do to me, Father," De adds.

"I am sorry, son. This is a decision that I could not make. I am not powerful enough to go against the seniors and Amy's father. Our lives are long, so to us, it will be quick."

"No, I cannot see Amy with someone else, having a family and being with another."

"And I do not want another."

"I am truly sorry. You will wake from the accident, and live your life with no memories of De, or this place. You will remember everything when you return one day. Your father will meet you then and comfort you." His heart hurts as he sees his son holding onto Amy tightly, and Amy gripping onto De just as hard, tears streaming down her face.

Chapter Thirty-Six

Back to a New Reality

Sirens blare in the distance. Fire blazes all around. The cracking of plastic and metal snapping as men try to get into the car, as others try to extinguish the fire.

Blood pours from the bodies inside.

"We need to get them out. Two are bleeding badly; one female is crushed; and a male has been impaled. I cannot feel a pulse on them. There is a head injury on the other male that I can see. One young lady is thrown from the vehicle and is in critical condition."

It is chaos. There is a lorry on its side above the driver has a few scrapes, but he is otherwise unharmed. Police question him as the ambulance crew tries and assist the firemen.

The car is finally cut open, and the fire is out. The bodies are taken to awaiting ambulances. The paramedics try to resuscitate, but two remain unresponsive.

One male has a crushed skull, but he is alive. The female who is thrown has a heartbeat, but she is badly injured.

The other female who is crushed has no hope of being revived. The scene is one of mayhem. The lorry driver takes a corner too fast, flipping and hitting the small car, knocking it off the cliff and down a mountain.

The driver of the larger vehicle is sober but tired. He has been driving too long without a break and doesn't pay enough attention to his surroundings.

The small car hits a tree on the way down, the impact causing Amy to fly from the car; her seatbelt is unbuckled. She is reaching for a drink and takes it off for a second.

Julie is crushed as the car hits the tree, which then rolls further down the mountain after the initial impact.

Duke is impaled by a large branch, piercing his heart. Benny is hit by debris, cracking his skull instantly.

At the hospital, surgeons are waiting to try and save Amy and Benny. Amy has many broken bones and internal injuries. Benny loses a toe, as his feet has got stuck. He also has scratches all over, but his head is the main concern.

Julie and Duke are taken away to the morgue once the hospital has finished with them. Neither has parents who can be contacted or found.

In another part of the hospital, a lovely woman called Grace have given birth to a beautiful baby boy, her husband Mitchel by her side, pride showing on his handsome face.

The surgeons work tirelessly for hours on Benny and Amy. Finally, they manage to save them both.

Parents are called, and rooms are set up.

Amy's family is the first to arrive, both being terrified for their daughter. The tiny female looks so fragile in the large hospital bed.

One of the doctors arrives, introducing himself.

"I am Dr Eli. We are doing everything we can to help your daughter. She is strong and is fighting hard."

"That she is," Amy's dad agrees.

The doctor is young but capable. His dark blue eyes hold a kindness. Amy's mum has a good feeling about the handsome male smiles.

"Will she recover?" the mum asks.

"We are hopeful. Like I said she is strong."

Both parents then sit by Amy's bed holding her hands. Dr Eli looks over at the patient with warmth. Pushing his black hair back, he sighs and heads out, leaving the family alone.

Benny's parents take a while to get to the hospital. Having to find cover for their jobs.

On arrival, they find a nurse changing the bandages on his head. Still unconscious, he looks innocent. The doctor who is treating Benny explains things to them.

"The hit did some significant damage. We will know more when your son wakes. There is nothing more we can do except to wait."

"Thank you, doctor." Both Benny's parents politely reply. They then sit with their son, hoping that he will wake up soon.

It is a week before either shows any movement or signs of waking. Benny is the first to stir.

His mother sits beside him, and both of his parents take turns to be with him each day. Probably the longest time that each of them has spent with their son.

Gripping his mother's hand, Benny wakes. It takes him a while to completely open his eyes.

"Baby, you're OK. Take it slow. Let me get the doctor or a nurse."

"No, stay. Please," he tells his mother in a very groggy voice.

His mum obliges, squeezing his hand.

"Mum, I am so sorry. I have been a terrible son. Things will be better from now on. I promise. I love you."

"Oh, sweetheart. Just get better. You are my perfect, sweet, boy. Why say that? I love you, my baby."

Struggling to say more, Benny closes his eyes.

A nurse comes, taking his vitals. Calling the doctor when she is told about him awakening and talking.

"It is a good sign if he spoke. The doctor will be here shortly."

"Thank you, nurse."

In the other room, Amy also stirs. Her parents both are sitting by her side. Dr Eli also checking on her again. He is a very dedicated doctor.

Slowly, her eyes begin to open, looking around her. The doctor is at her side in an instant.

"Amy, I am Dr Eli; take it slow, and I shall explain everything to you."

"De?" Is all that comes from her.

"Honey, we are here," her mother gently tells Amy.

"Who is De, baby girl?" her dad asks.

"Dr Eli, De. It suits him. Isn't he handsome Mum?" Amy looks right at the doctor smiling. The pain relief is taking effect.

"Thank you, Amy. But I need to check you over. There was a lot of damage done to your body. Do you remember anything?"

"I remember you."

"About the crash."

"Crash? I am sorry, nothing comes to mind. My head is starting to hurt. All I can remember is flying, and your cobalt eyes."

"The doctor has been checking on you all week sweetheart."

"Oh, OK. Thank you, De. I mean, Dr Eli."

"You are more than welcome. I will let you be alone for a minute. I will come back to check you over and see how you are healing."

"Thank you, doctor," they all say at once.

"Mum, what happened? I am in pain, but how it came to be is a mystery."

"Baby, you had an accident. A lorry hit the car and you all went off a cliff. Benny is in a room down the corridor. As far as I know, he is doing OK. You had several surgeries. Dr Eli fixed you up. He has been very good."

"It is starting to come back. Not the accident but being in the car. We were going to a hotel for a trip. It was a unique place. But the name escapes me."

"That is OK. It will come back. Your brain has probably blocked out the worst. It was a bad fall."

"Julie and Duke. Are they here?"

"Baby, I don't want to stress you more. When the doctor has checked you over, we can talk about the rest. OK."

The family chat for a while longer. The doctor returns and looks over Amy. She is healing well.

Meanwhile, Benny isn't doing well. His body is fine and the injury to his head. But he isn't responding to anyone now. Only crying and shaking.

This goes on for a long time. His father is now with them, and both parents are worried.

"Benny, it's Dad. Talk to us, son. What is going on? You weren't at fault. The lorry driver was."

"Dad, I am sorry. So many bad things. I was not a good guy. So many. Why didn't I stop? I hurt Dad. The pain in my heart is worse. Mum, please help me. Make the thoughts stop coming."

"Benny, sweetheart. What do you mean? Come back to us, baby." His mother begs.

The doctor explains that the injury to his head may have changed his personality. Old Benny may be gone.

Checking him over, the doctor isn't concerned.

"He may need psychological help now, but his injuries are healing well."

Chapter Thirty-Seven

Three Months Later

It has been a while since the accident. Amy is recovering at home with her parents. She has decided to become a nurse after being in the hospital for so long. Being near Dr Eli had nothing much to do with her decision.

Speaking of Dr Eli, or De as Amy likes to call him, has been a frequent visitor. The pair become close friends, Amy develops real feelings for the handsome man.

A physiotherapist often visits with Dr Eli, Amy's movement greatly improving.

As for Benny. He has been seeing someone. His family couldn't be with him, so Benny was put into a place to help with his mental difficulties. After talking to specialists, his mind was starting to heal.

Wanting to be better, he has decided to become a social worker. Helping kids with problems. He also wants to find people from his past, to make amends with what he did. Starting with the red-headed beauty he hurt badly.

New Lives

It has taken Benny a long time to complete his mission, but he finally became a social worker. Being very good at his job, going above and beyond.

After finding the young girl with the red hair, Benny became smitten with her. She remembered the day he hurt her but forgave him after knowing the man he has become.

Benny is working on getting her to date him.

His other victims are not so easy to find. The girls who are caught in the burning playhouse are from different parts of the world. Benny couldn't tell them what he did, but he wanted to help in any way he could.

Both had scars from the incident. Benny paid for surgeries to try and fix them, he also got them therapy. The money he had saved went to the victims of his past, not wanting fancy things anymore.

The beautiful girl takes her own life because of him; that is difficult. She has a little sister. So he makes sure that her life is full. Telling her about the sister that she doesn't get to meet and helping the parents with small things. Whatever he could do.

Donations are made to animal shelters and different charities. Benny has also adopted several dogs that he spoils rotten.

Amy becomes the nurse she wanted to be, working alongside her husband Dr Eli.

After learning about the death of her friends, she decides to make the most of her life. Grasping everything with both hands, Dr Eli is one of them.

They get married a year after the accident, Dr Eli proposing over dinner at her favourite restaurant. Their love is epic; some might say they are a perfect match.

Amy has a great job, her colleagues being amazing.

"Amy, we are looking at taking Sarah away for the weekend before the treatment starts." Sarah is a good friend who works with them. She has recently been diagnosed with a brain tumour.

"That sounds great; she will love it. I will cover for you. Just make sure she has fun."

"You, Amy, are an angel. We have found this place that looks a little different. It is called the Circle House."

Epilogue

Well, isn't that interesting. There are a few loose ends.

Yes, Dr Eli is my son. I couldn't let him be alone for that long, so he is given a mortal life to be with Amy, and then they will join us.

Benny stays true to his word; he becomes a better man each day.

You may have noticed that only a few names are mentioned. Well, the focus is on the main characters. If they are named, then their story is important.

In our world, names hold power, and they can be used against us.

Julie is here; she hasn't changed her ways yet. Maybe she never will.

Duke is growing into the sweetest person. His heart is as big as that personality. Having better parents made a big difference.

Amy's father was extremely angry with us for hurting her. I see everything, but her identity was hidden by him. Because my son is matched with Amy, we were given a warning; our seniors were also warned.

Seniors are like council members. They assist us in hard decisions. Beings that are ghosts of previous leaders. Voices that float around, reviewing all.

We have come to an end. Although a path never stops, journeys carry on.

Remember that your path may have someone watching.

Am I watching?